HAPPY ARE THE HAPPY

ALSO BY YASMINA REZA

PLAYS

"Art"
The God of Carnage
Life x 3
The Unexpected Man
Conversations after a Burial

FICTION

Desolation

NONFICTION

Dawn Dusk or Night:
A Year with Nicolas Sarkozy

Happy Are the Happy

YASMINA REZA

TRANSLATED FROM THE FRENCH
BY JOHN CULLEN

OTHER PRESS
NEW YORK

Production Editor: Yvonne E. Cárdenas
Text Designer: Julie Fry
This book was set in Bembo and Gill Sans.

10 9 8 7 6 5 4 3

Library of Congress Cataloging-in-Publication Data
Reza, Yasmina.
   [Heureux les heureux. English]
   Happy are the happy / by Yasmina Reza ; translated from
the French by John Cullen.
      pages cm
      ISBN 978-1-59051-692-8 (hardcover)—ISBN 978-1-59051-693-5
(ebook)
   1. Man-woman relationships—Fiction. 2. Adultery—Fiction.
I. Cullen, John, 1942– translator. II. Title.
   PQ2678.E955H4813 2014
   843'.914—dc23
                                          2014005643

for Moïra

Felices los amados y los amantes
y los que pueden prescindir del amor.
Felices los felices.

Happy are those who are beloved and those who love
and those who can do without love.
Happy are the happy.

— JORGE LUIS BORGES

1 ROBERT TOSCANO

9 MARGUERITE BLOT

15 ODILE TOSCANO

22 VINCENT ZAWADA

29 PASCALINE HUTNER

36 PAOLA SUARES

44 ERNEST BLOT

51 PHILIP CHEMLA

57 LOULA MORENO

63 RAOUL BARNÈCHE

70 VIRGINIE DÉRUELLE

77 RÉMI GROBE

85 CHANTAL AUDOUIN

92 JEAN EHRENFRIED

99 DAMIEN BARNÈCHE

106 LUC CONDAMINE

113 HÉLÈNE BARNÈCHE

119 JEANNETTE BLOT

127 ROBERT TOSCANO

140 ODILE TOSCANO

148 JEAN EHRENFRIED

Robert Toscano

We were at the supermarket, shopping for the weekend. At some point she said, you go stand in the cheese line while I get the rest of the groceries. When I came back, the shopping cart was half filled with boxes of cereal and bags of cookies and packets of powdered food and other desserts. I said, what's all this for? —What do you mean, what's all this for? I said, what's the point of buying all this? —You have children, Robert. They like Chocolate Cruesli, they like Napolitains, they adore Kinder Bueno bars. She displayed the various packages. It's ridiculous to gorge those kids on sugar and fat, I said. This cart is ridiculous. She said, what kind of cheese did you buy? —A Crottin de Chavignol and a Morbier. And no Gruyère? she cried out. —I forgot and I'm not going back, the line's too long. —If there's one kind of cheese you have to buy, you know very well it's Gruyère, who eats Morbier in our house? Who? I do, I said. —Since when do you eat Morbier? Who wants to eat Morbier? Odile, stop it, I said. —Who likes this Morbier crap? Implicit meaning: *besides your mother*, my mother had recently found a nut, a metal nut, in a chunk of Morbier. I said, Odile, you're shouting. She gave the cart a jerk and threw three Milka chocolate bars into it. I picked them up and replaced them on the shelf. She flung the bars back into the cart even faster than before. I said, I'm out of here. She answered, get out, get out, I'm out of here is all you know how to say, it's your sole response. As soon as you run out of arguments, you say I'm out of here, you immediately resort to this grotesque threat. It's true, I admit it, I often say I'm out of here, I'm aware I say it, but I don't see how I can not say it when it's the only thing I want to say, when I see no way out other than immediate withdrawal, but I also realize, yes, that I put it in the form of an ultimatum. Well, you're finished shopping, I say to Odile, propelling the shopping cart forward. Or do we have some more stupid shit to buy? —Listen to the way you talk to me! Do you even realize how you talk to me? I say, come on. Come on! Nothing irks me more than these sudden mood shifts, where everything stops, everything freezes. Obviously, I could say I'm sorry. Not just once, I'd have to say it twice, in the right tone. If I said I'm sorry, if I said it twice in the right tone, then the day could restart and almost return to normal, except that I don't in the least feel like saying those words, nor is there any physiological possibility of my uttering them when she stops short in front of shelves of condiments with that flabbergasted look of outrage and desolation. Come on, Odile, please, I say more gently. I'm cold and I have an article to finish. Apologize, she says. If she said *Apologize* in her normal voice, I might comply, but she whispers, she gives the word a colorless, atonal inflection I can't get past. I say, please. I remain calm. Please, I say mildly, and I see myself driving down a highway at top speed, stereo turned all the way up, and I'm listening to a song called "Sodade," a recent discovery I understand nothing of except for the solitude in the singer's voice and the word *solitude* itself, repeated countless times, even though I'm told *sodade* doesn't actually mean solitude, but nostalgia, absence, regret, spleen, so many intimate things that can't be shared, and all of them names for solitude, just as the personal shopping cart is a name for solitude, and so is the oil and vinegar aisle, and so is the man pleading with his wife under the fluorescent lights. I say, I'm sorry. I'm sorry, Odile. Odile's not necessary in that sentence. Of course not. Odile isn't nice, I say Odile at the end to indicate my impatience, but I don't expect her to make an about-face, arms dangling, and head for the frozen foods, that is, for the back of the store, without saying a word, leaving her handbag in the shopping cart. I shout, what are you doing, Odile? I shout, I've got only two hours left to write a very important article on the new gold rush! A completely ridiculous declaration. She's disappeared from sight. People are looking at me. I grab the handle of the cart and make a beeline for the back of the store. I don't see her (she's always had a talent for vanishing, even from pleasant situations). I call out, Odile! I go to the beverage section: nobody. Odile! Odile! I'm clearly upsetting the people around me, but I couldn't care less, I wheel the cart up and down the aisles—I loathe these supermarkets—and suddenly I spot her in the cheese line, which is even longer than it was a little while ago, she's got herself back in the cheese line! I go up to her and say, Odile, I express myself in a measured tone, Odile, I say, it's going to be twenty minutes before you get served, let's leave and buy the Gruyère somewhere else. No response. What's she doing? She digs around in the shopping cart and pulls out the Morbier. You're not going to return the Morbier? I ask. —Yes I am. We'll give it to Maman, I say, trying to lighten things up. My mother recently found a metal nut in a chunk of Morbier. Odile doesn't smile. She remains stiff and offended, standing there in the penance line. My mother said to the cheesemonger, I'm not the type of woman who makes a fuss, but for the sake of your longevity as a respected dealer in cheese, I must inform you that I found a bolt in a piece of your Morbier. The guy didn't give a damn, he didn't even offer to comp the three Rocamadours she was buying. My mother boasts that she paid without flinching, thus proving herself a bigger person than the cheesemonger. I stand close to Odile and say in a low voice, I'm counting to three, Odile. I'm counting to three. You understand? And for some reason, at the moment when I say that, I think about the Hutners, a couple of friends of ours who are curled up together inside a willed state of conjugal well-being. Lately they've taken to calling each other "my own" and saying things like "Let's eat well this evening, my own." I don't know why the Hutners cross my mind at the moment when an opposite madness has come over me, but maybe there isn't really a whole lot of difference between *Let's eat tonight, my own*, and *I'm counting to three, Odile*, in both cases the effort to be a couple causes a kind of constriction of the being, I mean there's no more natural harmony in *Let's eat well, my own*, no, not at all, and no less disaster either, except that my *I'm counting to three* causes a shiver to pass over Odile's face, a wrinkling of the mouth, the infinitesimal beginnings of a smile, while I must absolutely refrain from beginning to smile myself, of course, as long as I don't receive an unequivocal green light, even though I really feel like smiling, but instead I've got to act as if I haven't noticed a thing, and so I decide to count, I say *one*, I whisper the word distinctly, the woman right behind Odile has a ringside view, Odile pushes a bit of discarded packaging with the tip of her shoe, the line's getting longer and not moving at all, it's time for me to say two, I say *two*, openly, generously, the woman behind Odile practically glues herself to us, she's wearing a hat, a kind of overturned bucket made of soft felt, I can't stand women who wear that sort of hat, a hat like that's a very bad sign, I put something in my look intended to make the woman back off a yard or so, but nothing happens, she considers me curiously, she sizes me up, does she smell disgustingly bad? Women who dress in layers often give off a bad odor, or could it be the proximity of spoiled dairy products? My cell phone vibrates in my inside jacket pocket. I screw up my eyes to read the caller's name because I don't have time to find my glasses. It's a colleague with a tip about the Bundesbank's gold reserves. To cut the conversation short, I tell him I'm in a meeting and ask him to send me an e-mail. That little phone call may prove to be a stroke of luck. I lean down and murmur into Odile's ear, in the tone of a man returning to his responsibilities: my editor in chief wants a sidebar on German gold reserve stockpiling, it's something of a state secret, and that call may point me to information I don't have at the moment. German gold reserves, she says, who cares about that? And she pulls in her neck and draws down the corners of her mouth so that I can gauge the insignificance of the subject, but even more seriously, the insignificance of my work, of my efforts in general, as if there was no hope of expecting anything more from me, not even the consciousness of my own derelictions. Women will seize any opportunity to deflate you, they love reminding you how much of a disappointment you are. Odile has just moved up in the cheese line. She's got her bag back, and she's still clutching the Morbier. I'm hot. I'm suffocating. I want to be far away, I no longer remember what we're doing here or why we're doing it. I'd like to be sliding on snowshoes in western Canada, planting stakes and marking trees with my ax in frozen valleys, like the gold prospector Graham Boer, the subject of my article. Does this Boer person have a wife and children? A guy who confronts grizzly bears and temperatures of twenty-five below zero isn't likely to put up with being bored to death in a goddamn supermarket at grocery rush hour. Is this any place for a man? Who can wander up and down these fluorescent rows, past this plethora of packaging, without yielding to discouragement? And to know that you'll be back here, in all seasons of the year, whether you want to or not, hauling the same shopping cart, under the command of a woman who grows more rigid every day. Not long ago, my father-in-law, Ernest Blot, told our nine-year-old son, I'm going to buy you a new pen, you're staining your fingers with that one. Antoine replied, that's all right, I don't need a pen to be happy anymore. There's the secret, Ernest said, the child understood it: reduce your requirements for happiness to a minimum. My father-in-law is a champion of over-the-top adages totally out of keeping with his actual temperament. Ernest has never given in to the smallest reduction in his vital potential (forget the word *happiness*). When he was compelled to live like a convalescent after his coronary bypass operations, faced with relearning modest everyday routines and performing domestic chores he'd always avoided, he felt as though he'd been singled out and struck down by God himself. Odile, I say, if I say three, if I speak the number *three*, I'll take the car and leave you here on your own, shopping cart and all. Seems unlikely, she says. —It may seem unlikely, but it's what I'm going to do in two seconds.

—You can't take the car, Robert, the keys are in my bag. I rummage in my pockets, a gesture made all the more stupid by the fact that I remember handing her the keys. —Give them back, please. Odile smiles. She slings her bag across her shoulders and wedges it between her body and the Plexiglas front of the cheese display case. I move closer, grab the bag, and pull on it. Odile resists. I yank the shoulder strap. She clutches it and pulls the other way. She's having fun! I seize the bag by the bottom, I wouldn't have any trouble snatching it away from her if circumstances were different. She laughs. She clings. She says, aren't you going to say *three*? Why don't you say *three*? She's getting on my nerves. And those keys in her bag, they're getting on my nerves too. But I really like Odile when she's like this. I really like to see her laugh. I'm on the verge of relaxing and letting our struggle turn into a kind of teasing game when I hear a chuckle, and then I see the woman in the felt hat, giddy with feminine complicity, burst out laughing without the slightest embarrassment. All at once, I have no choice. I become brutal. I flatten Odile against the Plexiglas and try to get my hand inside her bag. She struggles, complains that I'm hurting her, I say, give me those fucking keys, she says, you're crazy, I tear the Morbier out of her hands and heave it into the aisle, at last I feel the keys amid the general disorder of her bag, I take them out, I wave them in front of her eyes without letting her go, I say, let's get the hell out of here *this minute*. Now the woman with the hat is looking scared. I say to her, what's the matter, honey, you're not laughing anymore? Why not? I pull both Odile and the cart, I haul them along past the shelves and the racks toward the checkout counters. I keep a tight grip on her wrist even though she's not putting up any resistance, there's nothing innocent about her submission, I'd rather she forced me to drag her. Whenever she dons her martyr's costume, I always wind up paying the price. Of course, the checkout lines are long too. We take our place in one deadly queue without exchanging a word. I release Odile's arm. She pretends to be a normal customer. I even watch her organize the shopping cart, arranging things a little to make them easier to bag. Our mutual silence continues in the parking lot. Also in the car. Night has fallen. The streetlights make us drowsy, and I put on the CD with the Portuguese song, the one with the woman's voice repeating the same word over and over.

Marguerite Blot

In the distant era of my marriage, in the hotel where we used to go as a family in the summer, there was a woman we would see every year. A cheerful, elegant woman with a sporty cut to her gray hair. She appeared everywhere, moving from group to group and dining at a different table every evening. Often, late in the afternoon, she could be found sitting with a book. She'd settle herself into a corner of the lounge so she could keep an eye on the comings and goings. Whenever she saw anyone who looked the least bit familiar, her face would light up and she'd wave her book like a handkerchief. One day she arrived with a tall brunette woman wearing an airy pleated skirt. Afterward, they were never seen apart. They had lunch on the lakeshore, played tennis, played cards. I asked who the tall woman was. *Une dame de compagnie*, I was told: a lady companion. I accepted the designation as one accepts an ordinary word, a word without a specific connotation. The two women appeared every year at the same time, and I'd say to myself, there's Madame Compain and her lady companion. In due course, a dog was added to their party. They'd take turns holding its leash, but the animal clearly belonged to Madame Compain. We'd see all three of them stepping out every morning, the dog pulling the ladies forward as they strove to hold it back by modulating its name through all the keys, but without any success. In February this past winter, and therefore a great many years later, I went on a mountain holiday with my son, who's a grown man now. He skis, of course, with his friends, and I walk. I love to go on walks, I love the forest and the silence. The staff at the hotel suggested some trails I could take, but they were all too far away and I didn't dare. One shouldn't walk too far alone in the mountains and the snow. I laughed, thinking that I ought to put up an ad at the reception desk: Single woman seeks someone pleasant to walk with. Anyway, I immediately thought about Madame Compain and her lady companion, and I understood what it meant to be *une dame de compagnie*. My understanding frightened me, because Madame Compain had always struck me as a woman who was a bit lost. Even when she was laughing with other people. And maybe, now that I think about it, especially when she was laughing, and also when she was dressing for the evening. I turned to my father—that is, I raised my eyes to heaven—and murmured, Papa, I can't become a Madame Compain! It had been a long time since I'd last spoken to my father. Since he died, I've been asking him to intervene in my life. I look up at the sky and talk to him in a secret, vehement voice. He's the only person I can speak to when I feel powerless. Besides him, I don't know anyone in the next world who would pay me any attention. It never occurs to me to address God. I've always thought you can't disturb God. You can't speak to him directly. He doesn't have the time to get involved with individual cases. Or if he does, they have to be exceptionally serious. On the scale of entreaties, mine are, in a manner of speaking, absurd. I feel the way my friend Pauline did when she lost a necklace she'd inherited from her mother and then found it in some tall grass. As they were passing through a village later, her husband stopped the car and rushed over to the church. It was locked, and so he started frantically rattling the door handle. What are you doing? Pauline asked. I want to thank God, he replied. —God doesn't give a shit! —I want to thank the Blessed Virgin. —Listen, Hervé, think about the size of the universe, think about the countless evils on earth, think about all the things that happen down here. If there's a God, if there's a Blessed Virgin, do you really believe my necklace matters to them?... And so I address my father, who seems more accessible. I ask him for specific favors. Maybe because circumstances make me desire specific things, but also because—below the surface—I want to gauge his abilities. It's always the same call for help. A petition for movement. But my father's hopeless. Either he doesn't hear me or he has no power. I find it appalling that the dead have no power. I disapprove of this radical division of our worlds. From time to time I attribute prophetic knowledge to my father. I think: he's not granting your wishes because he knows they won't be conducive to your welfare. That upsets me, I feel like saying, mind your own business, but at least I can consider his nonintervention a deliberate act. That was what he did with Jean-Gabriel Vigarello, the last man I fell in love with. Jean-Gabriel Vigarello is one of my colleagues, a professor of mathematics at the Lycée Camille-Saint-Saëns, where I myself teach Spanish. In retrospect, I tell myself my father wasn't wrong. But what's retrospect? It's old age. My father's heavenly values exasperate me. They're quite bourgeois, if you think about them. When he was alive, he believed in the stars, haunted houses, and all sorts of esoteric baubles. My brother Ernest, despite the way he makes his unbelief a cause for vanity, resembles our father a little more every day.

Recently I heard him repeat in his turn, "The stars incline us, they do not bind us." I'd forgotten how much our father adored that slogan, to which he'd add, almost threateningly, the name of Ptolemy. I thought, if the stars don't bind us, Papa, then what could you possibly know about the immanent future? I became interested in Jean-Gabriel Vigarello on the day I noticed his eyes. It wasn't easy to spot them, given that he wore his hair very long and it totally concealed his forehead—a hairstyle at once ugly and impossible for someone of his age. I thought at once, this man has a wife who doesn't take care of him (he's married, naturally). You don't let a man who's pushing sixty wear his hair like that. And most importantly, you tell him not to hide his eyes. Color-changing eyes, sometimes blue, sometimes gray, and shimmering like a mountain lake. One evening I found myself alone with him in a café in Madrid (we'd organized a school trip to Madrid with three of our classes). I got my nerve up and said, you have very gentle eyes, Jean-Gabriel, it's pure madness to keep them hidden. After that statement and a bottle of Carta d'Oro, one thing led to another and we wound up in my room, which overlooked a courtyard with howling cats. Once we were back in Rouen, he immediately replunged into his normal life. We'd cross paths in the halls of the lycée as if nothing had happened. He always seemed to be in a hurry, carrying his schoolbag in his left hand, his whole body leaning to that side and his graying bangs covering up more of his face than ever. I find it pathetic, the silent way men have of sending you back in time. As if it was necessary to remind us, for future reference, that human existence is fragmented. I thought, I'll write a note and put it in his mailbox. An inconsequential, witty note, containing a reference to an incident in Madrid. I stuck the note in his box one morning when I knew he was there. No response. Not on that day, and not during any of the following days. We greeted each other exactly as before. I was assailed by a kind of sadness, I can't say heartache, but rather the sorrow of abandonment. There's a poem by Borges that begins, *Ya no es mágico el mundo. Te han dejado.* The world's not magical anymore. You've been left. He says *left*, an everyday word, a word that makes no noise. Anybody can leave you, even a Jean-Gabriel Vigarello, who wears his hair like the Beatles fifty years after. I asked my father to intervene. In the meantime, I'd written another note, a single phrase: "Don't forget me completely. Marguerite." That *completely* struck me as ideal for dissipating his fears, if he had any. A little reminder in a jesting tone. I told my father, I still look good, but as you can see, nothing's up, and soon I'm going to be old. I told my father, I leave the lycée at five in the afternoon, right now it's nine in the morning, you've got eight hours to inspire Jean-Gabriel Vigarello with a charming reply that I'll find in my mailbox or on my cell phone. My father didn't lift a finger. In retrospect, I see that he was right. He's never approved of my absurd infatuations. He's right. You choose some faces from among others, you set out markers in time. Everybody wants to have some tale to tell. In former days, I launched myself into the future without thinking about it. Madame Compain was surely the type to have absurd infatuations. When she used to come to the hotel alone, she'd bring a great deal of luggage. Every evening she put on a different dress, a different necklace. She wore her lipstick even on her teeth, which was part of her elegance. She'd go from one table to the next, drinking a glass with one group and then another with another, always animated, always making conversation, especially with men. At the time, I was with my husband and children. In a little warm cell, from which one looks out at the world. Madame Compain fluttered around like a moth. In whatever corners the light reached, however feebly, Madame Compain would appear with her lacy wings. Ever since my childhood, I've made mental images for time. I see the year as an isosceles trapezoid. Winter's on top, a confident straight line. Fall and spring are attached to it like a skirt. And the summer has always been a long flat plain. These days I have the impression that the angles have softened and the figure's not stable anymore. What's that a sign of? I can't become a Madame Compain. I'm going to have a serious talk with my father. I'm going to tell him he has a unique opportunity to manifest himself for my welfare. I'm going to ask him to reestablish the geometry of my life. It's a matter of something very simple, very easy to arrange. Could you—this is what I'm preparing to say to him—could you put some lighthearted person in my way, someone I can laugh with and who likes to go on walks? Surely you know someone who'd keep the ends of his scarf crossed and smoothed flat under an old-fashioned coat, who'd hold me with a solid arm and lead me through the snowy forest and never get us lost.

Odile Toscano

Everything gets on his nerves. Opinions, things, people. Everything. We can't go out anymore without the evening ending badly. I find myself persuading him to go out, yet on the whole I almost always regret it. We exchange idiotic jokes with our hosts, we laugh on the landing, and once we're in the elevator, the cold front moves in. Someday someone should make a study of the silence that falls inside a car when you're returning home after having flaunted your well-being, partly to edify the company, partly to deceive yourself. It's a silence that tolerates no sound, not even the radio, for who in that mute war of opposition would dare to turn it on? This evening's over, we're home now, and while I undress, Robert, as usual, is dawdling in the children's room. I know what he's doing. He's checking their breathing. He bends over them and takes the time to verify unequivocally that they aren't dead. Afterward, we're in the bathroom, both of us. No communication. He brushes his teeth, I remove my makeup. He goes to the toilet room. A little later, I find him sitting on the bed in our bedroom; he checks the e-mails on his BlackBerry and sets his alarm. Then he slips under the covers and immediately switches off the light on his side of the bed. For my part, I go and sit on the other side, I set my alarm, I rub cream into my hands, I swallow a Stilnox, I place my earplugs and my water glass within reach on the night table. I arrange my pillows, put on my glasses, and settle down comfortably to read. I've hardly begun when Robert, in a tone that's supposed to be neutral, says, please turn out the light. These are the first words he's spoken since we were on Rémi Grobe's landing. I don't answer. After a few seconds pass, he raises himself and leans across me, half lying on me, in an effort to reach my bedside lamp. He manages to switch it off. In the darkness, I hit him on the arm and the back—actually I hit him several times—and then I turn the light on again. Robert says, I haven't slept for three nights, do you want me dead? Without raising my eyes from my book, I say, take a Stilnox. —I don't take fucking sleeping pills. —Then don't complain. —Odile, I'm tired...turn off the light. Turn it off, dammit. He curls up under the covers again. I try to read. I wonder whether the word *tired* in Robert's mouth hasn't contributed more than anything else to our drifting apart. I refuse to give the word any existential significance. If a literary hero withdraws to the region of shadows, you accept it, but the same doesn't go for a husband with whom you share a domestic life. Robert switches on his lamp again, extricates himself from the bedclothes with uncalled-for abruptness, and sits on the edge of the bed. Without turning around, he says, I'm going to a hotel. I remain silent. He doesn't move. For the seventh time, I read, "By the light filtering through the dilapidated shutters, Gaylor could see the dog lying under the toilet chair, the chipped enamel washbasin. On the opposite wall, a man looked at him sadly. Gaylor approached the mirror..." Now who exactly is Gaylor? Robert's leaning forward, his back to me. He maintains that position while he says, what do I do wrong, do I talk too much? Am I too aggressive? Do I drink too much? Do I have a double chin? Come on, let's have the litany. What was it this time? Well, you certainly talk too much, I say. —It was so damned boring. And disgusting. —It wasn't great, that's true. —Disgusting. What the hell does he do, this Rémi Grobe? —He's a consultant. —Consultant! he exclaims. Who's the genius who invented that word? I don't see why we inflict these ridiculous dinners on ourselves. —You're not obliged to go to them. —Yes I am. —No you're not. —I most certainly am. And that dumb bitch in red, the one who didn't even know that Japan doesn't have the atomic bomb! —What does it matter? Who needs to know that? —When you don't know anything about Japan's military defenses, and who does, then you shouldn't join in a conversation about territorial claims in the China Sea. I'm cold, I want to pull up the comforter, but it's stuck under Robert, who inadvertently sat on it. I tug at the comforter. He lets me try to pull it out from under him without lifting himself an inch. I haul on it, groaning slightly. It's a mute and completely idiotic struggle. In the end, Robert gets up and leaves the room. I turn to the preceding page to figure out who Gaylor is. Robert reappears fairly quickly. He's got his pants back on. He looks for his socks, finds them, puts them on. He leaves the room again. I hear him in the hall, opening a closet and rummaging around. Then he goes back into the bathroom, or so it seems to me. On the preceding page, Gaylor's in the back of a garage, arguing with a man named Pal. Who's this Pal? I get out of the bed, step into my slippers, and join Robert in the bathroom. He's wearing an unbuttoned shirt and sitting on the side of the bathtub. I ask him, where are you going? He makes a desperate gesture that means I don't know, it makes no difference. I say, do you want me to fix up a bed for you in the living room?

—Don't worry about me, Odile, go to bed. —Robert, I have four hearings this week. —Please leave me alone. I say, come back to bed, I'll turn off the lamp. I see myself in the mirror. Robert's got the bad lights on. I never use the ceiling lights in the bathroom, or if I do, I turn them on together with the spotlights over the washbasin. I say, I look ugly, she cut my hair too short. Much too short, Robert says. That's Robert's style of humor: half teasing, half disturbing. It's supposed to make me laugh, even in the worst moments. And it's also supposed to disturb me. I say, are you serious? Robert says, how can that jackass be a consultant? In what? —Who are you talking about? —Rémi Grobe. —In art, in real estate, I don't know exactly what. —A dabbler with his fingers in everything. A bandit, most likely. He's not married? —Divorced. —Do you think he's good-looking? We hear a sliding sound in the hall, followed by a little voice: Maman? What's wrong with him? Robert asks me, as if I knew, and in the instantly anxious tone that sets my teeth on edge. We're here, Antoine, I say, Papa and I are in the bathroom. Antoine appears, dressed in his pajamas and practically weeping. —I lost Doudine. Again! I say, are you going to lose Doudine every night? You shouldn't be worrying about Doudine at two in the morning, Antoine, you should be sleeping! Antoine's face crumples in slow motion. When his face crumples like that, there's no way of stopping his tears. Robert asks, why are you bawling him out, the poor kid? That question requires me to call upon my entire capacity for self-control. I say, I'm not bawling him out, but I don't understand why he doesn't put Doudine on a leash. She can just be tied up during the night! I'm not bawling you out, sweetie, but this is not the time to worry about Doudine.

Come on, let's go back to bed. We head for the boys' bedroom. Antoine's sniffling, *Doudiiine*, as Robert and I march down the hall in single file. We enter the bedroom. Simon's asleep. I ask Antoine to calm down so he won't wake up his brother. Robert whispers, we're going to find her, little hamster. Are you going to tie her up? Antoine whines, not making the least effort to lower his voice. I'm not going to tie her up, little hamster, Robert says. I switch on the bedside lamp and say, but why not? We can tie her up at night in a way that will be very pleasant for her. She won't feel a thing, and you'll have a little piece of string, like a little leash, and you can pull on it when... Antoine starts to wail like a siren. Few children can achieve such an exasperating command of plaintive modulation. Shh, shhh, I say. What's going on? Simon asks. —There! Now you've waked up your brother, bravo! —What are you all doing? Doudine's lost, Robert says. Through half-closed eyes, Simon looks at us like we're crazy. He's right. I crouch down to peer under the bed. Since I can't see much, I start running my hand all over the bottom of the bed. Robert's rummaging in the comforter. With my head under the bed, I mutter, I can't understand why you're not asleep in the middle of the night! That's not normal. When you're nine years old, you sleep. All of a sudden, I feel her, jammed between the slats and the mattress. I've got her, I've got her, I call out. Here she is! Quite a pain in the ass, this Doudine... Antoine presses the stuffed animal against his mouth. —All right, beddy-bye! Antoine gets into his bed. I kiss him. Simon wraps himself up in his covers and rolls over, turning away like someone who's just witnessed a distressing scene. I switch off the lamp. I try to push Robert out of the room. But Robert stays. He wants to compensate for Mother's harshness. He wants to reestablish harmony in the enchanted room of childhood. I watch him bend over Simon and kiss him on the back of the neck. Then, in darkness I've increased as much as possible by leaving the door just barely ajar, he sits down on Antoine's bed, tucks him in, nestles the comforter around him, and wedges Doudine so she can't escape. I hear him murmuring tender words and wonder whether he's starting one of the stories about Master January's forest. In former times, men would leave to hunt lions or conquer territories. I wait on the threshold, jerking the door back and forth from time to time to make my irritation known, even though the marmoreal position I've adopted should be sufficiently eloquent. Robert finally stands up. We traverse the hall again, in silence. Robert goes into the bathroom, I go into the bedroom and get back in bed. I turn over. I put on my glasses. "Pal was sitting at his desk. His plump hands rested on the dirty blotter. He was informing Gaylor that Raoul Toni had come into the garage that very morning..." Who's Raoul Toni? My eyes are closing. I wonder what Robert can be doing in the bathroom. I hear a footstep. He appears. He's removed his pants. How often can this particular threat be made in the course of a married life, this madness of dressing and undressing? I say, do you think it's normal for a nine-year-old to still have a cuddly toy? Of course, Robert says. I still had one when I was eighteen. I feel like laughing but I don't show it. Robert takes off his socks and his shirt. He turns off his bedside lamp and slips under the covers. I think I know who Gaylor is. Gaylor's the guy who's been hired to find Joss Kroll's daughter, and I have a hunch Raoul Toni has appeared already too, at the raffle in the beginning... My eyes close. This thriller is not thrilling. I remove my glasses and switch off the light. I turn so that I'm facing the night table. I notice I haven't pulled the curtain far enough over, it's going to let the light in too early. Too bad. I say, why does Antoine wake up in the middle of the night? Robert replies, because he can't feel Doudine. We both stay where we are for a while, each on one side of the bed, staring at the opposite wall. Then I turn over, once again, and press myself against him. Robert puts his hand on the small of my back and says, I ought to tie you up too.

Vincent Zawada

While waiting for her radiation therapy session at the Tollere Leman clinic, my mother scrutinizes every patient in the waiting room and says, in a barely lowered voice, wig, wig, not sure, not a wig, not a wig…Maman, Maman, not so loud, I say, everybody can hear you. What are you saying? my mother asks. You're muttering under your breath and I can't understand you. —Have you turned your ear on? —What? —Where's your hearing aid? Why don't you have it on? —Because I have to take it off during the radiation. —Put it on while we're waiting, Maman. It's no use, my mother says. The man sitting next to her gives me a sympathetic smile. He's holding a Prince of Wales beret in his hands, and his pale complexion is in keeping with his outdated, English-style suit. In any case, says my mother, digging around in her purse, I don't even have it with me. She goes back to people-watching and hardly lowers her voice when she says, that one there, she won't last a month. Notice, I'm not the oldest person here, that's reassuring… Maman, please, I say, here, look, there's a fun quiz in *Le Figaro.* —All right, if it makes you happy. —What vegetable previously unknown in France did Queen Catherine de' Medici introduce to the court: artichoke, broccoli, or tomato? Artichoke, my mother says. —Artichoke, right, good. What was Greta Garbo's first job when she was fourteen: barber's assistant, lighting double for Shirley Temple in *Little Miss Marker*, or herring-scaler at the fish market in

Stockholm, her native city? Herring-scaler in Stockholm, my mother says. —No, barber's assistant. Oh, right, says my mother, how stupid of me, since when do herring have scales! If I may be so bold, madam, they've had them a very long time, says the man sitting next to her. I notice his tie, gray with pink polka dots, as he explains, herring have always had scales. Really? says my mother. No, no, herring don't have scales, they're like sardines. Sardines have always had scales as well, the man says. Sardines have scales, news to me, says my mother. Did you know that, Vincent? Like anchovies and sprats, the man adds. In any case, I deduce from this conversation that you don't keep kosher! He laughs and includes me in his attempt at familiarity. In spite of his yellowing teeth and his sparse, graying hair, he has a certain style. I nod my head amiably. Fortunately, my mother says, fortunately I don't keep kosher. As if it's not enough that I don't have any appetite anymore anyway. Who's your doctor? the man asks, loosening the knot in his polka-dot tie a little and arranging his body for conversation. Doctor Chemla, my mother says. Philip Chemla, the best, there's nobody better, he's been keeping me going for six years, says the man. And me for eight, says my mother, proud of having been kept going longer. Lung too? the man asks. Liver, my mother answers, first breast and then liver. The man nods like someone who knows the song. But I'm atypical, you see, my mother goes on, I don't do anything the same as everybody else, every time Chemla sees me, he says, Paulette—he calls me Paulette, I'm his pet patient—he says, you're completely atypical, translation: you should have croaked a long time ago. My mother laughs heartily, and so does the man. As for me, I wonder whether a return to the quiz isn't well overdue. He's really a wonderful doctor, my mother goes on—by now she's beyond all control—and I find him personally very attractive too. The first time I saw him I said, are you married, Doctor? Do you have children? No children, he said. I said, you want me to show you how it's done? I press her hand, dry and withered from her medications, and I say, Maman, listen. What? says my mother, it's true, he was delighted, he laughed his head off, I've rarely seen an oncologist laugh like that. The man nods approvingly and says, he's a true gentleman, Chemla is, a real mensch. One day, I'll never forget it, he said these words to me, he said, when someone steps into my office, he honors me. Do you know he's not even forty? My mother couldn't possibly care less about any of that. She pursues her own line, as if she hasn't heard a thing the man said. Last Friday, she goes on, speaking louder and louder, I told him, Doctor Ayoun—he's my cardiologist—is a much better physician than you are. That'll be the day, says Chemla. Oh, but he is, I say, he complimented me right away on my new hat, but you, Doctor, you haven't even noticed it. I feel I must move. I get up and say, Maman, I'm going to ask the receptionist how much longer you have to wait. My mother turns to her new friend and says, he's going to smoke, my son's going outside to smoke a cigarette, that's what that means. Tell him he's slowly killing himself, and him only forty-three. Ah well, that way we'll die together, Maman, I say. Look on the bright side. Very funny, says my mother. The gentleman in the polka-dot tie pinches his nostrils and inhales like a man preparing to deliver a decisive communication. I cut him short to explain that I'm not going out for a smoke, even though a nicotine fix would do me a world of good, I'm just going to talk to the receptionist. When I return, I inform my mother that her radiation will start in ten minutes and that Doctor Chemla has not yet come into the office. Ah, that's just like Chemla, he and his watch don't get along, he can't imagine that we might have a subsidiary existence outside this office, says the man, happy to let the sound of his voice be heard again and hoping to hold the floor. But my mother returns to the attack at once and declares, I'm on the best of terms with the receptionist, she always puts me at the top of the list, I call her Virginie. My mother lowers her voice somewhat and adds, she adores me, I say to her, be a sweetheart and give me the first appointment, my dear Virginie. She's delighted by that, that personal touch. Vincent, my love, shouldn't we bring her some chocolates next time? Why not, I say. —What? You're muttering under your breath. I say, it's a good idea. We should have been able to get rid of Roseline's *vanillekipferl* before now, my mother says, I haven't even opened the box. She doesn't know how to make them, you think you're eating sand. Poor Roseline, these days she quivers like a bunch of keys. You know, she's a different woman since her daughter disappeared in the tsunami, one of the twenty-five bodies that have never been recovered, and Roseline believes she's still alive. Sometimes that irritates me, I feel like telling her, sure, right, she's being raised by chimpanzees that have given her amnesia. I say, don't be mean, Maman. —I'm not mean, but sometimes you have to be fatalistic, everybody knows the world's a vale of tears. Vale of tears, one of your father's expressions, you remember? I answer, yes, I remember. The man in the polka-dot tie seems to be lost in some rather somber thoughts. He's bending forward, and I notice a crutch lying beside his chair. It occurs to me that he's suffering in some part of his body, and I tell myself that other people in this waiting room on the basement floor of the Tollere Leman clinic must also be suffering in secret. You know, says my mother abruptly, leaning toward the man with an amazingly serious look on her face, my husband was obsessed with Israel. The man straightens up and smoothes the creases in his pinstripe suit. Jews are obsessed with Israel, but not me, my mother goes on. Me, I'm not at all obsessed with Israel, but my husband was. I'm having trouble following my mother along this tangent. Unless she's trying to correct the misimpression caused by the scaleless fish. Yes, that's it, maybe she wants to make it clear that her whole family is Jewish, including her, despite her ignorance of some fundamental dietary laws. Are you obsessed by Israel too? my mother asks. Naturally, the man replies. I approve of his concision. If I had my way, I could discourse at some length on the profundity of that reply of his. My mother, however, has a different apprehension of things. When I met my husband, she says, he had nothing at all, his family ran a notions shop on Rue Réaumur, a tiny place, a real dump. By the end of his life, he was a wholesaler, he owned three warehouses and an apartment building. And all that, he wanted to leave all that to Israel. —Maman, what's got into you? What's this tale you're telling? It's the truth, my mother says, without even taking the trouble to turn in my direction, we were a very close, very happy family, the only black spot was Israel. One day I told him the Jews didn't need a country and he almost hit me. Another time, he threw Vincent out of the house because he wanted to take a trip down the Nile. The man prepares to make a remark, but he's not fast enough. By the time he opens his pallid lips, my mother has already segued into Chemla wants to give me a new treatment, I can't take Xynophren anymore, my hands are falling into shreds, as you see. He wants me to have another round of chemo, a chemo drip this time, which is going to make me lose all my hair. Maman, that's not certain, I say, Chemla said one chance out of two. One chance out of two means two chances out of two, my mother says, sweeping aside my statement with a gesture, but I don't want to die like they did in Auschwitz, I don't want to face my end with a shaved skull. If I have this treatment, it's good-bye to my hair. And at my age, I don't have enough time for it to grow back. And it's good-bye to my hats, too. My mother shakes her head and mimes distress. She's been holding herself bolt upright while talking nonstop, stretching her neck out like a pious young girl at prayer. I don't delude myself, you know, she says. I'm here in this dreadful room, chatting with you, but only as a favor to my sons and Doctor Philip Chemla. I'm his pet patient, he enjoys taking care of me. Just between us, these radiation treatments are useless, they do no good whatsoever. They're supposed to make me see as well as I used to, and every day my eyes are worse. Don't say that, Maman, I say, the doctor explained that the treatment wouldn't produce immediate results. What are you saying? my mother asks, you're muttering under your breath. The results aren't instantaneous, I repeat. Not instantaneous means not guaranteed, my mother says. The truth is that Chemla's not certain about anything. He's groping around. I'm his guinea pig, fine, someone has to do it. I'm a fatalist. When my husband was on his deathbed, he asked me whether I was still an enemy of Israel, the homeland of the Jewish people. I answered, but no, of course not. What do you say to a man who's not going to be around much longer? You tell him what he wants to hear. It's strange to cling to such idiotic values. In your final hour, when everything's about to disappear. A homeland, who needs a homeland? After a while, even life is an idiotic value. Even life, don't you think? my mother says with a sigh. The man reflects. He could make a reply, because my mother seems to have suspended her babbling, and on a curiously meditative note. But at that instant a nurse calls for Monsieur Ehrenfried. The man grabs his crutch, his Prince of Wales beret, and a Loden overcoat that's lying on the chair next to him. Still seated, he leans toward my mother and murmurs, life, maybe, but not Israel. Then he braces himself on his crutch and laboriously gets to his feet. Duty calls, he says, bowing, I'm Jean Ehrenfried. It was a pleasure. You can tell that every movement is quite difficult for him, but he continues to show a smiling face. The hat you're wearing today, he says, is that the one that elicited compliments from your cardiologist? My mother touches her hat to verify her answer. No, no, she says, this one's the lynx. The one I wore to Doctor Ayoun's office is a kind of Borsalino with a black velvet rose. The man says, my compliments on the one you're wearing today, it brought a touch of class to this waiting room. It's my little lynx toque, says my mother flirtatiously. I've had it for forty years, does it still look good on me? It looks perfect, says Jean Ehrenfried, saluting her with a whirl of his beret. We watch him walk away and disappear behind the door to the radio-therapy room. My mother thrusts her bruised hands into her purse. She pulls out a compact and a lipstick and says, he's got a bad limp, the poor man, I wonder if he hasn't fallen in love with me.

Pascaline Hutner

We didn't see this coming. We never imagined things could fall apart this way. Never. Not Lionel, not me. We're alone and confused. Who can we talk to about it? We ought to talk about it, but a secret like this—who could we tell it to? We ought to be able to discuss it with people we trust, with very compassionate people who wouldn't so much as suggest that they found anything humorous in it. We don't tolerate the smallest hint of humor on the subject, although we're well aware, Lionel and I, that we might laugh about it if it didn't involve our son. Actually, given the slightest inducement, we'd probably laugh about it in company. We haven't even told Odile and Robert. The Toscanos have been our friends forever, despite the fact that it's not so easy to maintain a friendship between couples. An in-depth friendship, I mean. In the end, the only truly intimate relationships are those between two people. We should have seen one another in twos, separately, just the women or just the men, or maybe even one of each (assuming that Robert and I would have managed to find anything to talk about in private). The Toscanos make fun of our mutual devotion. They've developed a certain attitude toward us, a kind of permanent irony that makes me tired. We can't say a word without them reacting like we're the very image of a congealed couple, suffocated by well-being. The other day, I made the mistake of saying that I'd prepared a turbot *en croûte* for dinner (I've been taking cooking classes, such fun). A turbot *en croûte*? Odile asked, as though I'd spoken in a foreign language. —Yes, a turbot cooked in a fish-shaped crust. —For how many people? Just for the two of us, I said, for Lionel and me, just for us two. Just for the two of you, that's scary! Odile said. Why? asked my cousin Josiane, who was with us. I could cook a turbot *en croûte* just for myself, she said. Just for yourself, all right, that takes on another dimension, Robert said, upping the ante. Cooking a turbot *en croûte*, a fish with a fish-shaped crust, just for yourself alone, that rises to the level of tragedy. As a rule, I play dumb to keep things from going downhill. Lionel doesn't give a damn. When I talk to him about it, he tells me the Toscanos are simply jealous, other people's happiness often seems somehow aggressive. If we were to describe what's happening to our family, I don't see how anyone could be jealous of us. But confessing the disaster that's befallen us is so hard precisely because we're such paragons of domestic felicity. I can just imagine the snide remarks people like the Toscanos would make if they knew. Let me back up a little and explain. Our son Jacob, who recently turned nineteen, has always loved the singer Céline Dion. I say always because this passion dates from when he was still a little boy. While riding in a car one day, the child heard Céline Dion's voice on the radio. Love at first sound. We bought that album for him and then the next one, the walls of his room got covered with posters, and—like a million other parents, I suppose—we found ourselves living with a little fan. Before long we were invited to concerts in his room. Jacob would dress like Céline in one of my slips and lip-synch her songs. I remember him unspooling some of the cassette tapes everybody had back then and using them to make himself a hairdo. I'm not sure Lionel thoroughly appreciated the show, but it was very amusing. At the time, we already had to put up with Robert's teasing—he'd congratulate us on our tolerance and open-mindedness. But it was very amusing. As Jacob got older, he gradually stopped being satisfied with merely singing like Céline; he started speaking like her and giving interviews to absent interviewers in a Canadian accent. He'd do Céline, and he'd do her husband René, too. It was funny. We'd laugh. Jacob imitated her to perfection. We'd ask him questions, I mean, we'd talk to Jacob and he'd answer as Céline. It was very amusing. It was really very amusing. I don't know what went wrong. How did we go from a childish passion to this... I don't know what to call it... to this derangement of his spirit? Of his very being?... One evening when all three of us were at the kitchen table, Lionel told Jacob he was tired of listening to him and his Québécois clownery. I'd made salt pork and lentils, a little dish my two men were usually crazy about, but this time there was something sad in the air. It was like the feeling you get when you're alone with someone and the other person withdraws into himself and you see that withdrawal as an omen of abandonment. Jacob pretended not to know the meaning of the word *clownery*. He replied to his father in Québécois French, declaring that although he'd been living in France for some time, he was a Canadian woman who had no intention of disavowing her origins. Raising his voice, Lionel said Jacob's act was getting to the point where it wasn't funny anymore, and Jacob answered that he couldn't keep up this "squabbling" because he had to protect his vocal cords. After that awful night, we started living with

Céline Dion in Jacob Hutner's body. We were no longer called Papa and Maman, but Lionel and Pascaline. And we no longer had any relationship with our real son. At first we thought we were dealing with a temporary crisis, one of those little delirious phases teenagers go through. But when Bogdana, our cleaning lady, came and told us that Jacob had very graciously (she was on the point of finding him too good-natured for such a major star) requested a humidifier for his voice, I sensed that things were taking a turn for the worse. Without saying anything to Lionel—sometimes men are too prosaic—I consulted a magnetic therapist. I'd heard about people being possessed by entities. The magnetic therapist explained that Céline Dion wasn't an entity and that therefore he wasn't in a position to disengage her from Jacob. An entity is a vagabond soul that attaches itself to a living person. The therapist couldn't liberate a boy inhabited by someone who sang in Las Vegas every night, he said, and he advised me to make an appointment with a psychiatrist. The word *psychiatrist* stuck in my throat like a cotton-wool plug. A certain amount of time had to pass before I felt capable of uttering that word at home. Lionel proved to be more realistic. I would never have been able to get through this trial without Lionel's stability. Lionel. My husband. My own. True to himself, never pushy, never inclined to devious ways. One day Robert said Lionel was a man on the lookout for joy, a man in search of happiness, but happiness of a "cubic" kind. We laughed at this roguish remark, and I even gave Robert a little slap. But all things considered, he had a point: cubic. Solid. Upright on every side. We got Jacob to see a psychiatrist by persuading him that the doctor was an ear, nose, and throat specialist. The psychiatrist recommended a stay in a private hospital. I was shattered when I saw how easily our child could be manipulated. Jacob strode cheerfully into the mental clinic, convinced that he was entering a recording studio, a kind of studio-hotel reserved for stars of his stature so they wouldn't have to go back and forth every day. When we stepped into the bare, white room on that first morning, I came near to falling at his feet and begging his forgiveness for such treachery. We've told everybody that Jacob has left the country to do an internship abroad. Everybody, including the Toscanos. The only person in on the secret is Bogdana. She persists in baking him Serbian cakes with walnuts and poppy seeds, even though he never touches them, for Jacob no longer likes what he used to like before. He remains normal physically, he doesn't imitate a woman. His condition is something that goes much deeper than mere imitation. Lionel and I have wound up calling him Céline. In private, we sometimes even refer to him as "she." Doctor Igor Lorrain, the psychiatric physician who's treating our son in the clinic, tells us that Jacob's never unhappy except when he watches the news. He's obsessed by the arbitrary nature of his good fortune and privileged status. The nurses talk about taking away his television because he cries straight through all the evening news programs, even stories about a harvest wiped out by a hailstorm. And there's also another aspect of his behavior that worries the psychiatrist. When Jacob goes down to the lobby of the clinic to sign autographs, he first wraps several scarves around his neck so he won't catch cold. He has his world tour to think about, the doctor jokingly explains (I'm not crazy about that doctor). Jacob positions himself in front of the revolving door, convinced that the people who enter the hospital have traveled great distances just to see him. When we arrived yesterday afternoon, he was at his post. I could see him from the car before we turned into the parking lot. He was visible through the glass panels of the revolving door, bending down toward a child, looking absurdly friendly, and scribbling something in a little notebook. Lionel knows my silences well. After parking the car, he looked at the plane trees and asked, is he downstairs again? I nodded and we hugged each other, unable to speak. Doctor Lorrain tells us Jacob calls him Humberto. We've explained that he probably takes him for Humberto Gatica, his sound engineer—well, I mean Céline's sound engineer. Which is logical enough, if you think about it, because both of them look like Steven Spielberg. In the same way, we've heard Jacob call the nurse from Martinique Oprah (as in Oprah Winfrey), whereupon she starts wriggling as though she feels flattered. Today was such a difficult day. First he said to us, using that pronunciation I'll never be able to imitate, you don't look very happy at the moment, Lionel and Pascaline. I have a lot of empathy for other people, and it upsets me to see you like this. Would you like me to sing something to cheer you up? We said no, he needed to rest his voice, he already had enough work to do with cutting his records, but he insisted all the same. He sat us down side by side, just the way he used to do when he was little, Lionel on a stool and me in the leatherette armchair. And then, standing in front of us and demonstrating a fine sense of rhythm, Jacob sang us a song called "Love Can Move Mountains." When he was finished, we did what we used to do when he was a little boy: we burst into loud applause. Lionel put one arm around my shoulders to keep me from weakening. Evening came, and as we were walking down the corridor on our way out of the clinic, we heard people calling out to one another in Canadian French. Hey, David Foster, take a look at this! Has Humberto come down yet? Ask Barbra! That one should go on a two-year break, too! Then we heard them laughing, and we realized that the nursing staff was making fun of Céline and her entourage. Lionel couldn't take it. He went into the room where the laughter was coming from and said in a solemn voice that sounded silly even to me, I'm Jacob Hutner's father. There was a silence. Nobody knew what to say. And so I said, come on, Lionel, it doesn't matter. And the nurses started mumbling apologies. I tugged at my husband's sleeve. Disoriented, no longer sure where the elevator was, we went down some stairs that echoed under our footsteps. Outside it was nearly dark and raining a little. I pulled on my gloves and Lionel headed for the parking lot without even waiting for me. I said, wait for me, my own. He turned around, squinting through the raindrops, and I saw how very small his head looked and how thin his hair was in the light of the streetlamp. I thought, we have to return to our normal life, Lionel has to go back to his office, we have to stay cheerful. After we got in the car, I said I felt like going to the Russian Canteen and drinking vodka and eating piroshki. And then I asked him, who do you suppose Barbra is? Barbra Streisand, Lionel said. —Yes, but in the clinic. Do you think she's the head nurse with the long nose?

Paola Suares

I'm very sensitive to light. I mean psychologically. I wonder if everybody's sensitive to light this way or if I'm particularly vulnerable. I can put up with exterior light. I can put up with dismal weather. The sky's there for everyone. All men and women go through the same fog. Interiors return you to yourself. Light in enclosed spaces attacks me personally. It strikes objects, it strikes my soul. Certain lights deprive me of all sense of the future. When I was a child, I ate in a kitchen that looked out onto a closed courtyard. The illumination that came from the ceiling made everything gloomy and gave me the feeling of having been forgotten by the world. When we got to the central hospital of the Tenth Arrondissement, where Caroline had just had her baby, it was around eight in the evening. I suggested to Luc that he should go up with me, but he declined and said he preferred to wait in the car. He wanted to know if I was going to be long, and I said, no, no, even though the question seemed a bit out of place, not to mention uncouth. It was raining. The street was empty, likewise the lobby of the maternity ward. I went to the room and knocked on the door. Joel opened it. Pale and happy, Caroline was sitting on the bed in a dressing gown and holding a tiny infant, a little girl, in her arms. I bent over her. She was pretty. Very delicate, really very pretty. I had no problem saying so and congratulating them. The room was exceedingly warm. I requested a vase for the anemones I'd brought. Joel told me flowers were forbidden in the rooms. I'd have to keep my bouquet. I removed my coat. Caroline handed the baby to her husband and got into bed. Joel took the little bundle in his arms and sat down on the imitation leather armchair, nodding his head, puffed up with papahood. Caroline took out a Jacadi catalog and showed me a foldable baby travel bed. I made a note of the item. On a Formica shelf, there were some packages, still half-wrapped, and several bottles of hydroalcoholic gel. I asked if there was an intensive care unit in the building, because I was on the verge of a heat stroke. Caroline said they couldn't open the windows because of the infant and offered me some discolored fruit paste candies. A disposable baby bottle and a crumpled baby blanket lay in the transparent crib. The strange ceiling light made all the cloths, sheets, napkins, and bibs look yellow. A life was beginning in this confined, indescribably dreary world. I stroked the sleeping baby's forehead, I kissed Joel and Caroline. Before leaving the building, I put the anemones, which were drooping from the heat, on a counter in the lobby. In the car, I told Luc that my friend's new daughter was really pretty. He asked, what are we doing? Shall we go to your place? And I said, no. Luc looked surprised. I said, I feel like a change. He turned on the ignition and started driving at random. I could tell he was miffed. —We always go to my place, I'm tired of being the easy option. Luc didn't reply. I shouldn't have said it that way. I regretted using the words *easy option*, but you can't control everything. Rain was still falling. We rolled along without speaking. He parked the car just ahead of the Place de la Bastille. We walked to a restaurant he knew. It was fully booked. Luc protested, but to no avail. We were already far from the car, and we'd wandered around quite a bit before finding a place to park. At one point, while we were still on the street, I said I was cold, and Luc said, let's go there. I could hear the irritation in his voice. —No, why there? —You're cold. We walked into a place I disliked on sight, and Luc immediately accepted the table the owner proposed. He didn't ask whether the choice suited me until we were taking our seats. The evening had already turned dicey, I didn't have the nerve to say no. He sat across from me, his elbows on the table, his hands crossed, his fingers at play. I was still feeling so cold that I couldn't take off my coat or my scarf. The waiter brought the menu. Luc pretended to be interested in it. His features looked drawn in the pale neon light. He got a text message on his cell phone from his youngest daughter and showed it to me: "We're eating a raklet!" His wife and children were on a mountain holiday. I begrudged Luc his lack of delicacy and incidentally found his parental doting pathetic. But I smiled amiably. I said, she's lucky. Luc said, yes she is. An emphatic yes. Nothing lighthearted about it. I was in no mood to figure out how to protect myself from that tone of voice. I said, aren't you joining them? —Yes, this Friday. I thought, he can go to hell. There was absolutely nothing on the menu that I could eat. Nor on any other menu in the world, in my opinion, and I said, I'm not hungry, I'd like just a glass of cognac. Luc said, I'm going to have the breaded veal escalope with fries. I was stricken by melancholy in this crummy, supposedly intimate booth. The waiter wiped the varnished table but stopped before it was really clean. I wonder if men suffer from this sort of attack without ever admitting it. I thought about the baby girl who was living through the first hours of her life, swaddled in her waxen room. A story occurred to me and I immediately told it to Luc by way of filling the silence. One evening at dinner, a psychiatrist—who's also a psychoanalyst—recalled the words of a patient of his, a man who suffered from solitude. This patient said to the psychoanalyst, when I'm home, I'm afraid someone will pay me a visit and see how alone I am. The analyst had added, sniggering a little, the guy's a broken record. I told Luc that part too. Luc was ordering a glass of white wine, and he sniggered exactly the way the psychoanalyst, Igor Lorrain, had sniggered—stupidly, and tediously, and appallingly. I should have walked out, I should have left him there in that absurd booth, but instead I said, I'd like to see where you live. Luc feigned astonishment and acted like a man who's not sure he understands. I repeated, I'd like to go home with you and see how you live. Luc looked at me as though I was getting interesting again and crooned, aha, home with me, my little hussy? I nodded in a vaguely mischievous way and immediately scolded myself for simpering like that, for being unable to stay my own course in Luc's presence. Nevertheless, I backed up a little (the waiter had just brought my glass of cognac) and said, you didn't like the story about the patient? You didn't understand it as a perfect allegory of absence? Luc said, absence from what? —From the other. —Oh, yes, yes, of course, Luc said, squeezing the mustard container. Are you sure you don't want to eat anything? At least take some fries. I took a fry. I'm not used to cognac or any strong liquor. My head starts to spin at the first swallow. It didn't even occur to Luc to take me to a hotel. He was so used to coming to my apartment that he couldn't conceive an alternate idea. Men are totally immobile creatures. We women are the ones who create movement. We wear ourselves out invigorating love. I've been going to a great deal of trouble ever since I met Luc Condamine. Some noisy young people, full of energy, occupied the booth behind ours. Luc asked me if I'd seen the Toscanos recently. We'd met at the Toscanos' apartment. Luc is Robert's best friend. They work at the same newspaper, but Luc's a senior correspondent. I said I'd been working late and hardly seeing anybody. Luc told me he'd found Robert depressed and so he'd introduced him to a girl. That surprised me, because I'd always thought that Robert was a different kind of man from Luc. I said, I didn't know Robert had affairs. —He doesn't, that's precisely why I'm arranging things for him. I reminded Luc that I was Odile's friend and he was giving me too much information. Luc laughed and wiped his mouth. He pinched my cheek with a semipitying look on his face. He'd already gobbled up his bowl of fried potatoes and was bearing down on the remains of his escalope. I asked, who is she? —Oh, no, Paola! You're Odile's friend, you don't want to know that! —Who is she? Do I know her? —No, you're right, it would be bad if you knew. —Yes, it would be very bad. So who is she? —Virginie. Medical secretary. —Where do you know her from? Luc made a sweeping gesture, indicating the vast world of his acquaintance. I felt cheerful all of a sudden. I'd drunk an entire glass of cognac in an unusually short time. But I was cheerful because Luc himself had brightened up at last. He ordered an apricot tart and two spoons. The tart was acidic and too creamy, but we fought over the last piece of fruit. The young people behind us were laughing, and I felt young like them. I said, will you take me home with you, Luc?

Let's go, he said. I couldn't tell whether this was a good idea anymore. In fact, my ideas were uniformly unclear. Things remained light for a little while. We ran through the rain. In the car, the mood was still light, at first. Then I dropped one of the CDs Luc kept in the center storage console. The disc slipped out of its case and rolled under my seat. When I came back up with the CD, Luc was already holding the case. Still driving, he took the CD out of my hands and put it back in its container himself. Then he stored it in its former place, tapping it a little to get the alignment right. All this was done without sound. Without words. I felt clumsy and maybe even guilty of an indiscretion. I could have considered the obsessiveness of his actions and deduced that Luc Condamine was a maniac, but instead I felt a stupid urge to cry like a child caught doing wrong. I no longer thought it was a good idea to go to his apartment. Once we were in the lobby of his building, Luc used his keys to open a glass door. On the other side there was a staircase with a baby carriage and a folded stroller hanging from the banister. Luc had me go ahead of him, and we climbed up to the fourth floor on stairs that wound around a shaft occupied by an invisible elevator. Luc turned on the lights in the entrance hallway of his apartment. I could make out some shelves with books and some coathooks where anoraks and overcoats were hanging. I took mine off, along with my gloves and my scarf. Luc showed me into the living room. He adjusted a halogen floor lamp and left me alone for a moment. As in every living room, in his there was a sofa, a low table, and a few mismatched chairs. A rather worn leather armchair. A bookcase with some books and framed photographs, among them one of Luc in the Oval Office, hypnotized by Bill Clinton. An assembly of haphazard elements. I sat in the leather chair, on the edge of the seat. The curtains were printed in a pattern I'd seen somewhere before. Luc came back. He'd taken off his suit jacket. He said, do you want something to drink? Cognac, I said, as if in the course of a single evening I'd become a woman who drank cognac at every given opportunity. Luc got a bottle of cognac and two glasses. He sat on the sofa and poured our drinks. He dimmed the floor lamp, turned on a smaller one with a pleated fabric shade, and sprawled backward on the sofa pillows, gazing at me. I was sitting on an inch or two of armchair, my back straight, my legs crossed, trying to give myself a Lauren Bacall air. Luc spread his legs and sank into the sofa. There was a sort of pedestal table between him and me, and on it stood a framed photograph of his wife, laughing with their two daughters, apparently at a miniature golf course. Luc said, Andernos-les-Bains. They have a family home in Andernos-les-Bains, near Bordeaux, which is where his wife's from. My head began to spin a little. Moving very slowly—I found him almost melodramatic—Luc started unbuttoning his shirt with one hand. Then he pulled the shirt open. I understood that the idea was for me to do the same thing, to strip off my clothes in the same slow rhythm a few feet away from him. Luc Condamine has a great hold over me in this regard. I was wearing a dress under a cardigan. I bared a shoulder. Then, to get ahead of him, I pulled off one cardigan sleeve. Luc took off one shirt sleeve. I took off the cardigan and threw it on the floor. He did the same with his shirt. Luc's upper body was naked. He was smiling at me. I pulled my dress over my head and rolled down one stocking. Luc removed his shoes. I took off my other stocking, knotted it into a ball and threw it at him. Luc unbuttoned his pants. I waited a little. He freed his sex, and all at once I realized that the sofa was turquoise. A turquoise that shimmered in the soft lamplight. Considering the rest of the room, I thought, it was rather surprising they'd chosen a sofa of that particular color. I wondered which member of this couple was responsible for interior decoration. Luc stretched out in a lascivious position I found both alluring and embarrassing. I looked around the room, at the pictures hanging in their false half-light, at the photographs, at the Moroccan paper lanterns. I wondered whose books these were, and whose guitar, and who claimed the horrible elephant's foot. You'll never leave all this, I told him. Luc Condamine raised his head and gazed at me as if I'd just said something immeasurably weird.

Ernest Blot

My ashes. I don't know what should become of them. Should they be shut up somewhere, or scattered? I ask myself this question while sitting in the kitchen in my bathrobe, my eyes fixed on the laptop computer. Jeannette comes and goes, like a woman glad to spread herself out on a holiday. She opens cupboards, turns on machines, rattles the cutlery. I'm trying to read the electronic version of a newspaper. I say, Jeannette, please! My wife replies, nobody forces you to occupy the kitchen the moment I start to make breakfast. A rumble of bad weather comes to us through the window. I feel worn out and stooped, I'm squinting in spite of my glasses. I gaze at my hand as it wanders the tabletop, clutching the tool called a *mouse*, part of my body's struggle with a world to which it no longer belongs. The other day my grandson Simon said, old folks are people from the past stuck in the future. That kid's a genius. The rain starts to beat against the windows and images come to me, images of the sea, of the shore, of ashes. My father was cremated and the remains placed in an ugly, square metal box. It was painted a shade of brown, the same color as the classroom walls in the Lycée Henri-Avril in Lamballe. My sister Marguerite, our two cousins, and I scattered the ashes from a bridge in Guernonzé. He wanted to be in the Braive. A hundred meters from the house where he was born. At six in the evening. In the middle of the town. I was sixty-four years old, a few months after my quintuple bypass. There's no spot that bears my father's name. Marguerite can't get used to the idea that he's not localized. When I go there—once a year, it's far away—sometimes I snatch a flower from somewhere nearby or sometimes I buy one, and in any case I toss it furtively. The flower floats away on the water. And I feel, for ten minutes, a sense of fulfillment. My father was afraid of being shut up like his brother. A brother who was the opposite of himself. A big-time gambler. A kind of Great Gatsby. When he went into a restaurant, the staff would grovel before him. He was cremated too. His last wife wanted to put him with her family, in the pharaonic tomb they have. An underling from the funeral home cracked open the engraved bronze door, set the urn on the first of the twelve marble shelves, and then closed the door again. As we were driving back from the cemetery, my father said, all your life you brag about your free access to high places, and then in the end they slip you inside through a crack in the door and plop you down at random. Me too, I'd like to merge with a flowing stream. But ever since I sold Plou-Gouzan L'Ic, I no longer have a river. And as for the river of my childhood, it's not very pleasant anymore. It used to be wild and unspoiled, grass grew between its rocks, a wall of honeysuckle ran its whole length. Now its banks have been paved over, and next to it there's a parking lot. In the sea, then. But it's too vast (and I'm afraid of sharks). I say to Jeannette, I'd like you to throw my ashes into a stream or a river, but I haven't chosen one yet. Jeannette stops the toaster. She wipes her hands on the dishcloth that's lying within reach and sits down in front of me. —Your ashes? Ernest, you want to be cremated? Too much consternation in her face. Too much pathos. I laugh, baring all my mean teeth, and say yes. —And you say it just like that, like you're talking about the weather? —It's not a significant topic of conversation. She remains silent. She smoothes the tablecloth and says, you know I'm against it. —I know, but I don't want to be stacked up in a vault, Jeannette. —You aren't bound to do everything just like your father, you're seventy-three. —That's the right age to act like one's father. I put my glasses back on. I say, would you be so kind as to let me read? You stick a dagger in me and then you go back to your newspaper, she answers. I'd be happy to see a newspaper appear on my screen, but I'm missing a password or some kind of identifier or something, how should I know? Our daughter Odile's taken it into her head to retrain me. She's afraid my brain will crumble away and I'll become isolated. When I was in business, nobody suggested I fall into step with modernity. Sinuous bodies flutter across the screen. They remind me of the flies that used to float before my eyes when I was a child. I talked about them to a little girl I knew. I asked her if they were angels. Yes, she said, they were. I felt a certain pride in them. I don't believe in anything. Certainly not in any kind of religious nonsense. But in angels, just a little. In the constellations. In my role, however minute, in the book of causes and effects. It's not forbidden to imagine that you're part of a whole. I don't know what Jeannette's doing, fooling around with that dishcloth instead of finishing the toast. She's twisting the corners of the cloth and wrapping them around her index finger. This distracts my attention completely. I can't have a serious discussion with my wife. Making myself understood is impossible. Particularly within the marital framework, where everything turns into a criminal case. Jeannette abruptly snaps the cloth off her finger and says lugubriously, you don't want to be with me. With you where? I ask. —With me in general. —But I do, Jeannette, I want to be with you. —No you don't. —Everyone's alone in death. And stop with that dishcloth, what are you doing? —I've always thought it was sad that your parents aren't buried together. Your sister thinks so too. Papa's very happy in the Braive, I say. And your mother is sad, says Jeannette. —My mother's sad! Once again I show my mean teeth. All she had to do was follow his example instead of having her parents' bones put into ossuaries to make room for her in the family tomb. Who made her do that? —You're monstrous, Ernest. —That's nothing new, I say. Jeannette would like us to be buried together so that passersby could see our two names. Jeannette Blot and her devoted husband, securely stashed away in stone. She'd like to erase forever the humiliations of our married life. In the past, when I'd stayed out all night, she'd rumple my pajamas before the housemaid arrived. My wife is counting on the grave to outfox spiteful gossips, she wants to remain a petit bourgeois even in death. The rain drums on the tiles. When I'd return from Bréhau-Monge to Lamballe, where my boarding school was, the evening breeze would be blowing. If raindrops streaked a windowpane, I'd press my nose against it. Renan says somewhere, "When the bell rings at five in the afternoon..." What book is that in? I'd like to read it again. Jeannette has stopped manipulating the dishcloth. She's gazing vacantly into space, into the gray weather. When she was young, she had a kind of impudent look about her. She resembled the actress Suzy Delair. Time changes everything, including the soul of a face. I say, don't I even get a cup of coffee? She shrugs her shoulders. In the old days, I never paid any attention to this dizzying loop of day and night, I wouldn't even know whether it was morning or afternoon or anything else. I'd go to the ministry, I'd go to the bank, I'd chase after women, I'd never worry about eventual consequences. I've still got enough joy left in me to do a little chasing, but after a certain age, the preliminaries are wearying. Jeannette says, you can also choose to be cremated without having your ashes scattered. I don't even react. I turn back to my false cybernetic activity. I'm not opposed to learning something new, but to what end? To stimulate my brain cells, my daughter says. Is that likely to change my worldview? There's already enough pollen and crap in the air without adding corpse dust, it's not worth the trouble, Jeannette says. I say, I'll ask someone else to do it—Odile, or Robert. Or Jean, but I'm afraid he's going to pass on before I do, that idiot. He wasn't looking very good last Tuesday. Throw me in the Braive. I'll rejoin my father. Just take care not to inflict any kind of ceremony on me, no funeral service or other foolishness, no tiresome blessed words. For all you know, I'll die before you, Jeannette says. —No you won't, you're robust. —If I die before you, Ernest, I want there to be a service with a blessing, and I want you to tell the story of how you proposed to me in Roquebrune. Poor Jeannette. In a distant time that's nothing more than a subject of confusion now, I asked her for her hand through the judas window of a medieval dungeon I'd shut her up in. If she only knew how utterly Roquebrune has lost all meaning for me. How that past has dissolved and turned into vapor. Two people living side by side, and every day their imaginations separate them more and more conclusively. Deep down inside themselves, women build enchanted palaces. You're mummified somewhere in there, but you don't know it. No licentiousness, no lack of scruples, no act of cruelty is considered real. The moment of eternal farewell arrives, and a story about two youngsters must be told. Everything is misunderstanding, and torpor. —Don't count on it, Jeannette. Happily, I'll disappear before you do. And you'll attend my cremation. And don't worry, that sort of thing doesn't smell like roasting pork the way it used to in bygone days. Jeannette pushes back her chair and stands up. She throws the dishcloth on the table. She turns off the gas stove—the water for my eggs has almost boiled off anyway—and unplugs the toaster. As she leaves the room, firing a parting shot, she says, good thing your father didn't choose to have himself chopped up in pieces, otherwise you'd want to be chopped up in pieces too. I think she turns off the ceiling light while she's speaking. There's hardly any light coming in from outside, and so I remain in darkness, good riddance to me. I take the pack of Gauloises out of my pocket. I promised Doctor Ayoun I'd stop smoking. Just as I promised him I'd eat salads and broiled steaks. A nice guy, that Ayoun. A single cigarette won't kill me. My eyes fall on the shrimp net with the wooden frame that's been hanging on the wall for decades. Fifty years ago, somebody used to plunge it under layers of seaweed and thrust it into rifts. In the old days, Jeannette would put bouquets of thyme, laurel, all sorts of herbs in that net. Objects pile up, items no longer of any use. And neither are we. I listen to the rain, which has dropped down a tone. The wind too. I lower the lid and close the laptop. All that our eyes can see is already in the past. I'm not sad. Things are made to disappear. I'll vanish without a fuss. There will be no coffin and no bones. Everything will go on as it has always done. Everything will float blithely away on the water.

Philip Chemla

I'd like to suffer for love. The other evening, in the theater, I heard these words: "Sadness after intimate sexual intercourse one is familiar with of course...Yes, that one knows and is prepared to face." The lines are from Beckett's play *Happy Days*. Oh, the happy days of sadness I've never known. I don't dream about a union or an idyll, I don't dream about any more or less durable romantic felicity, no, I'd just like to know a certain kind of sadness. I can guess what it's like. I may have already felt it. An impression halfway between a sense of something missing and a child's heavy heart. Among the hundreds of bodies I desire, I'd like to come across one with a talent for wounding me. Even from a distance, even absent, even lying on a bed beside me and turning away. I'd like to come across a lover armed with an indiscernible, flaying blade. That's the signature of love, I know it from the books I read long ago, before medicine stole all my time. Between me and my brother, there was never a word. When I was ten, he got into my bed. He was five years older than me. The door was ajar. I didn't understand very well what was going on, but I knew it was forbidden. I don't precisely remember the things we did. For years. Strokes and rubs. I remember the day he first came to me, and I remember my first orgasm. That's all. I'm not sure whether we kissed, but the place that sort of thing would eventually occupy in my life leads me to believe he must have kissed me. As time went on, and until his marriage, more and more it was I who approached him. No word passed between us. Except for his *No* when I presented myself. He'd say no, but he'd always give in. I remember only silences between us. No exchanges, no language meant to sustain an imaginary life. No coincidence of emotions and sex. We had a shed in the back of our yard. I'd go there and gaze out through a broken windowpane at the life in the street. One night a garbage truck driver spotted me and winked. The night was dark and the man inaccessible in his high cabin. Later, when I wasn't so young anymore, I'd go chasing after garbage men. My father, whose brother was in Guinea, had a subscription to the magazine *Vivante Afrique*. It was my first porn magazine. Matte bodies on matte paper. Stalwart, protective farmers, nearly naked, sparkling on the page. I hung a picture of Nefertiti on the wall above my bed. She kept watch like an icon, untouchable and somber. Before I went away to boarding school, I used to go to various public gardens and offer myself to Arabs there. I'd say, use me. One day when some guy and I were taking off our clothes in a stairwell, I sensed that he was going to swipe my cash. I said, you want some money? He melted into my arms. Things became simple, almost tender. My father is unaware of a big part of my life. He's an upright man, very attached to filial relationships. A genuine, good Jew. I often think about him. I feel freer since I started paying. My position is more legitimate, although I have to redress the power imbalance. I talk with some boys. I ask them questions about their lives, I show them respect. I address my father mentally, I say, well, there certainly is the occasional detour, but generally I stick to the main road. On Saturday evenings or sometimes during the week, after I'm through seeing patients and there are no meetings to attend, I go to the woods, or to the movie theaters in parts of town where the right kinds of boys can be found. I say to them, I like big dicks. I demand to see theirs. They pull it out. It's stiff or not. Recently, when I've chosen someone, I want to know if he's into slapping. (I don't offer to pay more for slapping. Slapping mustn't be part of the negotiation.) It used to be that I'd ask the question in the car. These days, I ask beforehand. It's an incomplete question. The entire question would be, will you hit me? And immediately afterward, will you comfort me? You can't ask that question. Nor can you say, comfort me. The farthest I can go is, stroke my face. I wouldn't dare say anything more. Some words have no place in such a setting. It's a strange command, *comfort me.* One can imagine giving all the other commands—lick me, hit me, kiss me, use your tongue (many don't)—but not *comfort me.* What I really want can't be stated. To be struck in the face, to offer my face to the blows, to present my lips, my teeth, my eyes, and immediately afterward to be stroked, caressed just when I least expect it, and then to be struck again, with the right rhythm, the just proportion, and after I come, to be embraced, supported, covered with kisses. Maybe that perfection doesn't exist outside the kind of love I don't know. Ever since I began to pay and thus became able to control the order of events, I'm free to be myself. I do what I can't do, and get what I can't get, in real life. I kneel, I abase myself. My knees sink into the earth. I return to total submission. Money binds us as well as any other attachment. The Egyptian put his hands on my face. He held my face, he pressed his palms against my cheeks. My mother did the same thing when I had an ear infection, she tried to cool my burning fever with her hands. Otherwise, in normal life, she was aloof. The Egyptian licked my mouth. He disappeared into the night, like the garbage collectors in days gone by. I walk along the side path, I plunge into the woods. He's not there. If I make an effort, I can still feel the dampness his tongue left on my lips. A dizzying summary of some knowledge I don't have. Jean Ehrenfried, a patient I've grown attached to, gave me a copy of Rilke's *Duino Elegies*. He said, a little poetry, doctor, would you by chance have time for that? He opened the book in front of me and read the first lines (I noted in passing that the timbre of his voice had thinned since his last visit): "If I cried out, then who among the angelic orders would hear me?" It's a small book. I keep it near my bed. I've reread those lines, thinking about Ehrenfried's diminished voice, about his combinations of polka-dot ties and fancy pocket handkerchiefs. For weeks those poems have been waiting under my bedside lamp. I get up at six-thirty every morning. I see my first patient an hour later. I can see around thirty in the course of a day. I teach, I write articles for international journals of oncology and radiation therapy, I go to fifteen or so conventions a year. I have no time to put my existence in perspective anymore. Sometimes friends drag me to the theater. I recently saw that Beckett play, *Happy Days*. A little umbrella under a dazzling sun. A woman whose body is sinking deeper and deeper, sucked into the earth. She wants to endure *lightheartedly* and rejoices in minuscule surprises. I know about that. I admire it every day. But I'm not sure I want to hear any other words. Poets have no sense of time. They draw you into useless melancholy. I didn't ask the Egyptian for his telephone number. I generally don't ask.

What good could come of it? Still, sometimes I get guys'
numbers. Not his. But he left a mark on me, something I
can't define. Maybe it has something to do with Beckett's
evil genius. The Egyptian isn't what I'm searching for in the
rendezvous spots behind the big worksite fence in Passy.
Although I even look for him in assignation rooms where
I've never seen him before, the thing I'm really seeking is
the smell of sadness. It's an impalpable thing, deeper than we
can gauge, and it has nothing to do with reality. My life is
beautiful. I do what I like to do. I get up in the morning
bursting with energy. I've discovered that I'm strong. I
mean, qualified to make decisions and take risks. My patients
have my cell phone number, they can call me at any time. I
owe them a lot. I'd like to be worthy of them (that's one of
the reasons why I want to keep up with the science and
carry on oncology research alongside my clinical practice).
I've known about the existence of death for a long time.
Before I started studying medicine, I could already hear the
clock ticking in my head. I bear no grudge against my
brother. As for his place in my life, I don't know exactly
what it was. Human complexity can't be reduced to any
causality principle. It may well be that had I not lived
through our years of silence, I would have had the courage
to face the abyss of a relationship comprising both sex and
love. Who can say? I generally pay afterward. Almost every
time. The other must trust me, as though offering a token of
friendship. But the Egyptian I paid beforehand. I took a
chance. He didn't put the bill in his pocket, he kept it in his
hand. That bill was in my field of vision all the while I was
sucking him. He put the bill in my mouth. I sucked his cock
and the money. He stuffed the banknote in my mouth and

put his hands on my face. It was a pledge with no tomorrow, a promise no one will ever know. When I was a child, I used to give my mother pebbles or chestnuts I'd find on the ground. I'd also sing little songs to her. Offerings at once useless and immortal. I've often had to convince patients that the present is the sole reality. The Egyptian boy put the banknote in my mouth and placed his hands on my face. I took everything he gave me, his cock, the money, the joy, the sorrow.

Loula Moreno

Anders Breivik, the Norwegian who shot sixty-nine people to death and killed eight others with a bomb, said during his trial in Oslo, "In normal circumstances I'm a very nice person." When I read that statement, I immediately thought of Darius Ardashir. In normal circumstances, when he's not applying himself to my destruction, Darius Ardashir is very nice. Apart from me, perhaps his wife, and the women who have had the misfortune of becoming attached to him, nobody knows he's a monster. The journalist interviewing me this morning is the kind of person who drinks her tea with careful movements while performing a series of irritating little rituals. Yesterday at around six in the evening, Darius Ardashir told me, I'll call you in fifteen minutes. My cell phone's on the table. No call, no text. It's noon. I nearly went crazy during the night. The journalist says, you've just turned thirty, do you have a wish? —I have a hundred wishes. —Pick one. I say, I'd like to play a nun. Or have wavy hair. Appalling answers. I'm trying to be witty. I don't know how to make simple, superficial small talk. —A nun! She produces a slightly twisted smile meant to affirm that I wouldn't be the first choice for such a role. —Why not? —What's your main fault? —I have a thousand faults. —The one you'd most like to get rid of. —My bad taste. —You have bad taste? In what? I say, men. And I immediately regret it. I always talk too much. A little girl, surely a schoolchild, is cleaning the table next to us. She moves the match holder, she places the pastries menu on another table, she wipes the waxed wood with a damp cloth, whirling her hand in deft, efficient circles; then she puts everything back where it was and goes away. From where I'm sitting, I can see her go to the bar and ask for another assignment. The real waitress gives her a tray of advertising cards folded in the shape of tents and points her to some empty tables. The young girl sets about putting a card next to the potted violet on each table. I love her seriousness. The journalist asks, do you prefer a certain type of man? I hear myself reply, I prefer the dangerous, irrational type. I filter that through a gurgle of laughter and say, I'm talking nonsense, Madame, please don't write that. —What a pity. —I'm not attracted by smooth, handsome guys, the *Mad Men* type, I like the little, dented ones, the kind that look bad-tempered and don't talk much. I could continue banging on like this, but I choke on an olive pit. I say, don't write down any of that. —I've already written it down. —Then don't publish it. Nobody's interested in that. —*Au contraire.* —I really don't want to talk about myself that way. —Our readers will be honored. You're giving them a gift. She readjusts her skirt under her bottom and asks for more hot water for her tea. I finish the olives and order a second glass of vodka. I let myself be reeled in, I have no authority over these people. The journalist asks me if I have a cold. No, I say, why? She finds my voice deeper in real life. She says I have bedroom intonations. I laugh stupidly. She thinks she's flattering me with that idiotic expression. My cell phone's still on the table, and still not giving any sign of life. None. Not one. The little girl is calmly walking back and forth among the sofas, her chin thrust well forward. —Loula Moreno, where does that come from? It's not your real name, is it? —I took it from a song by Charlie Odine...*Loula waits for her big day to come / In some drab impresario's bed, / Chews empty promises like gum, / With dreams of applause in her head*... —So does the big day come? —In the song? No. —Has it come for you? —Not for me either. I finish my vodka and laugh. It's wonderful that we can laugh. Laughter's like a joker. It works however you play it. The young girl's leaving. She's become a child again, with her raincoat and her schoolbag. At the moment when she disappears outside the glass-paned wooden door, I see Darius Ardashir come in. I knew he could sometimes be found in this bar. To tell the truth, I even chose the place deliberately, in the infinitesimal hope of seeing him. But Darius Ardashir isn't with his usual co-conspirators in their dark suits and ties (I've never understood exactly what it is that he does, he's the type of guy whose name is linked to politics one day and the next to an industrial group or an arms sale). He's with a woman. I empty my glass in one gulp, igniting my throat. I'm not used to drinking. The woman is tall, with a classic look to her and her hair in a blond chignon. Darius Ardashir guides her to two armchairs in the corner near the piano. His hair's wet. He's got his hand on the small of her back. I fail to hear the journalist's question. I say, I beg your pardon, I didn't get that. I raise my glass to a waiter and order another vodka. I say to the journalist, it wakes me up, I didn't get much sleep last night. I always have to justify myself. It's ridiculous. I'm thirty years old, I'm famous, I can dance on any precipice. Darius Ardashir's trying to close a little printed umbrella. He fights with the struts, brings no intelligence to the effort, and ends up crushing the thing together with brute force and then wrapping the fabric around the frame as best he can. The woman laughs. This spectacle is killing me. The journalist says, do you feel nostalgia for your childhood? By the way she's bending toward me, as one does with deaf people, I gather she must have asked me that question at least once already. Ah no, not at all, I say, I didn't like childhood, I wanted to be a grown-up. She leans even farther forward and says something I can't make out. I seize my cell phone, get up, and say, excuse me for a second. I head for the ladies' room as discreetly as possible, swaying a little because of the vodka. I look at myself in the mirror. I'm pale, I find the circles under my eyes a nice touch. I'm an attractive girl. I write a text on my phone, "I see you," and send it to Darius Ardashir. A few days ago, I told him I was his slave, I said I wanted him to keep me on a leash. Darius Ardashir answered that he didn't like encumbrances. Even a little suitcase disturbed him, he said. I return to the dining room carelessly. I don't look toward the piano. When the journalist sees me coming back, her face lights up with a practically maternal glow. She says, can we continue? I say yes and sit down. Darius Ardashir has surely received my message, I see him absorbed by his cell phone. I arch my back and stretch my swanlike neck. I must absolutely avoid looking in his direction. The journalist rummages in her notes and says, you said... —My God. —You said, men are love's guests. —I said that? Me? —Yes. —Not bad. —Can you expand on it? I say, will I get fussed at if I smoke? I'm afraid so, she says. My cell phone lights up. Darius A. is responding to my text: "Hey, sexy." I turn around. Darius Ardashir is ordering drinks. He's wearing a brown jacket over a beige shirt, the blond woman's in love with him, you can see that from miles away. *Hey, sexy,* as if nothing's going on. Darius Ardashir is a genius of the pure present. The night erases all traces of the previous day, and words start bouncing around again, as light as helium balloons. I text him: "Who is she?" I regret the text at once. I write, "No, I don't give a shit," but luckily I delete it. The journalist sighs and settles against the back of her armchair. I write, "We were supposed to have dinner last night, right?" I delete, delete. Reproaches make men take to their heels like sprinters. In the beginning, Darius Ardashir told me, I love you with my head, with my heart, and with my cock. I repeated that sentence to Rémi Grobe, my best friend, and he said, a poet, this guy of yours, I'm going to give that a try, there are some dopes it might work on. It works mighty well on me. I have no desire to hear music that's too subtle. I say to the journalist, what were we talking about? She shakes her head, she's no longer sure herself. My own head is spinning. I wave the waiter over and ask him to bring us more salted nuts, with extra cashews. I'm not going to leave that *Who is she?* hanging out there all by itself, it's too weak. Especially since he's not answering. I write, "Tell her you only like beginnings." That's excellent. I'm pressing send. No, I'm not pressing send. I can do better. I call the waiter over once again. He arrives with potato chips and nuts, a goodly portion of them cashews. I ask him for a piece of paper. I say to the journalist, excuse me, things are a little disjointed this morning. She raises a limp hand in a gesture of complete dejection. I don't have the time to be embarrassed. The waiter brings me a big sheet of typing paper. I ask him to wait. I write my sentence on the top part of the page and fold it with care. I ask the waiter to deliver the note discreetly, without disclosing its source, to the man in the brown jacket sitting next to the piano. The waiter says in a frightfully clear voice, Monsieur Ardashir? I flutter my eyelids in confirmation. He goes away. I fall on the mixed pistachios and cashews. I absolutely must not look at what's going on beside the piano. The journalist has roused herself from her torpor, taken off her eyeglasses, and stored them in their case. Now she's starting to put away her documents. I can't be abandoned there, not right away. I say to her, you know, I feel old. One doesn't feel young at thirty. Last night I couldn't sleep, and I read Cesare Pavese's journal. Do you know it? It's on my night table. Reading sad things is good for you. In one passage, he says, "Madmen and wretches have all been children, they played as you did, they believed something beautiful was waiting for them." Don't write this, but I've thought for a long time I wouldn't be anything more than a shooting star in this profession. The journalist looks at me nervously. She's nice, poor thing. The waiter comes back with the folded paper. I'm trembling. I keep it in my hand for a moment before unfolding it. There's what I wrote at the top, "Tell her you only like beginnings," and at the bottom, in a fine, black hand, he's written, "Not always". Nothing else. No period. To whom do those words refer? To me? To his wife? I turn my head toward the piano corner. Darius Ardashir and the woman are in a very good mood. The journalist leans toward me and says, something beautiful *was* waiting for you, Loula.

Raoul Barnèche

I ate a king of clubs. Not all of it, but almost. I am a man who reached such an extreme that I was capable of putting a king of clubs in my mouth and chewing part of it to pieces, munching and swallowing it the way a savage would munch and swallow raw flesh. I did that. I ate a card that had been handled by dozens of other people before me, and I did it in the middle of the annual bridge tournament in Juan-les-Pins. I admit only one error, the original mistake: playing with Hélène. Letting myself be taken in by the sentimental little song-and-dance women do. I've known for years that I shouldn't play with my wife as my partner anymore. The period when Hélène and I could play as a team, in a spirit of harmony—the word's an exaggeration and doesn't exist in bridge, let's say indulgence then, on my part in any case, or in a spirit of, I'm looking for the right word, of conciliation—that period is long gone. One day, by a stroke of luck, we won the French mixed open pairs championship together. Since then, our alliance has produced not a single spark and ruined my blood pressure. Hélène didn't know how to play bridge when I met her. A friend of hers brought her to a café where there were games at night. She was taking a secretarial course at the time. She sat down, she watched. She came back. I taught her everything. My father was an automotive toolmaker in a Renault plant and my mother a seamstress. Hélène came from the North. Her parents were textile workers. Nowadays things have become democratized, but in former times people like us wouldn't have been allowed into the clubs. Before I left everything for bridge, I was a chemical engineer at Labinal. I spent my days working in Saint-Ouen, my evenings at the Darcey in Place Clichy, and then in the clubs. Weekends at the racetrack. Little Hélène followed along. The passion for cards can't be communicated. There's a box in some brains, a box separate from the rest. It's the *Cards* box. Those who don't have it don't have it. You can take all the lessons in the world, there's nothing to be done. Hélène had it. In the short run, she played quite decently. Women can't concentrate for long periods of time. After thirteen years of playing bridge separately, one fine day Hélène woke up and suggested we go back to the Juan-les-Pins tournament and play together. Juan-les-Pins, the blue sky, the sea, the memory of a hotel in Le Cannet, God only knows what image she had in her head. I should have said no and I said yes, like every man who's growing old. The drama occurred at the seventeenth hand. North-South had reached a contract of five spades. My opening lead is the two of diamonds, dummy plays low, Hélène lays down the ace, declarer plays low. Hélène trots out her ace of clubs, North plays low, I have three clubs to the king, I play the nine, dummy plays low. So now what does Hélène do? What does a woman I've taught everything, a woman who's supposed to have become an elite player—what does such a woman do? She continues in clubs. I played the nine of clubs on the previous trick, and Hélène led another club! We had three sure tricks, and we made only two of them. At the end of the game, I showed her my king of clubs and cried, now where am I supposed to put this? Shall I eat it? Do you want to kill me, Hélène? Do you want me to have a heart attack right here in the middle of the Palais des Congrès? I waved the card under her nose and then stuffed the thing in my mouth. As I began to chew, I croaked at her, you saw my nine of clubs, you idiot, I played the nine, did you think I was playing it to pass the time? Hélène was petrified. Our opponents were petrified. That galvanized me. When you eat cardboard, the urge to vomit comes over you quite soon, but I worked my jaws aggressively and concentrated on mastication. I felt movement around us, I heard someone laugh, and I saw my friend Yorgos Katos's face coming my way. He was, like me, a veteran of the games in Place Clichy. Yorgos said, what the hell are you doing, Raoul, old boy, spit that crap out of your mouth. I said—with a great effort, because I was intent on getting that king of clubs down my gullet—I said, where did she put her white cane? Eh? Let's see that white cane, my poor girl! Raoul, Yorgos said, or so it seemed to me, you can't let yourself get so worked up over a bridge tournament, a bit of fun at the beach. Those are the last words I remember. I heard someone call the referee, the table was swaying, Hélène stood up, she extended her arms, I tried to catch her fingers, I saw her floating with the others in a circle above my head, I felt bodies close against mine, I retched, I puked on the card-table cover, and then everything stopped. I woke up in an anise green room that I didn't recognize and that turned out to be our hotel room. Three persons were whispering in the doorway. Yorgos, Hélène, and a stranger. Then the stranger left. Yorgos looked toward the bed and said, he's coming back to life. Yorgos has the same kind of hair as the novelist Joseph Kessel. A sort of lion's mane that appeals to women and makes me jealous. Hélène rushed to my bedside and said, are you all right? She gently stroked my forehead. I said, what's happening? —Don't you remember? You got a little hysterical yesterday evening at the tournament. Yorgos said, you ate a king of clubs. I ate a king of clubs? I asked, making what seemed like an immense but only partly successful effort to sit up. Hélène arranged my pillows. A ray of sunlight struck her face, she was as pretty as always. I said, my little Bilette. She smiled and said, the doctor gave you a shot to calm you down, Rouli (Bilette and Rouli are our private nicknames for each other). Yorgos opened the window. We heard children's cries and the music of a carousel. I don't know why, but deeply buried memories suddenly came back to me: the empty carousel in the seaside resort where my family used to go when I was a child, the barrel organ, the gray weather. We'd camp on the campground. I'd sit under the awning of the pump room, watching the animals go round and round and waiting for the end of the day. A violent sadness overcame me. I thought, uh-oh, what did that crazy doctor give me? I'll be going, Yorgos said. You have to stay in bed today. Tomorrow you can take a walk. A little nature will do you good, a few breaths of sea air, he said. The bar where we'd met, Yorgos and I, was on the corner of Place de Clichy and Boulevard des Batignolles. We were twenty years old. When the Darcey closed at two in the morning, we'd hurry over to Pont Cardinet. We lived our lives entirely without troubling ourselves about the light of day. From the club to the bed, and from the bed back to the club. We played all the games, poker, backgammon, we plucked quite a few pigeons in the back rooms. We amused ourselves with bridge and participated in big international championships. Yorgos was the last guy who should have been recommending nature and walks. Might as well prescribe the grave. I said, what happened? Is it serious? You don't remember anything, Rouli? Hèlène asked. I replied, not very clearly. Yorgos said, good luck, dear girl. He kissed Hélène and went out. Hélène brought me a glass of water. She said, you lost your temper at the end of a hand. —Why aren't we at the tournament? —We've been kicked out. I don't know what it is about carousel music, but that hurdy-gurdy sound can really give you a terrible case of the blues. I said, close the window, Bilette, and the curtains too, I'm going to sleep a little more. At around noon on the following day, I woke up for good at the moment when Hélène came back from the town with some packages and a new pink straw hat. She declared that I looked very well. She herself seemed enchanted with her purchases. She said, what do you think, it's not too big, is it? They also had some with plain ribbons, so I could exchange it, and in any case we have to go back to that store and buy you a hat too. I said, a straw hat like old men wear? What next? The sun's really beating down, Hélène said, you're not going to get a sunstroke on top of everything else. One hour later, I was sitting on the terrace of a café in the old town, wearing new glasses and a plaited hat. Hélène was perusing the tourist guide she'd bought, getting carried away at every page. Meanwhile I discreetly checked off the horses I liked in a copy of *Paris Turf* (I had permission to buy it, but not to consult it). She was the one who brought the matter up again. Out of the blue, she said to me, I didn't much appreciate your calling me an idiot in public, in front of everybody. —Did I call you an idiot, my Bilette? —In front of everybody. She made a little face like a vexed child. That really wasn't nice, I said. —And the white cane, that was truly hateful, you can't say, let's see that white cane, my poor girl, you can't say that to your wife, and in front of five hundred people. —Five hundred people, that's a bit of an exaggeration. —Everyone knows about it. —I wasn't myself, Bilette, you could see that. —All the same, it was pretty disturbing when you ate that card. I shrugged my shoulders and pulled in my neck the way a man who felt ashamed would do. It was hot. Various people passed by, adults wearing loose clothes and carrying canvas bags, children eating ice cream, girls covered with trinkets. I found I had nothing to say to Hélène. I watched the colorful, dismal parade. Hélène said, suppose we go and have a look at the Fort Carré? Or the archaeological museum? —All right. —Which one? —The one you prefer. —Maybe the archaeological museum. They have objects that were found in sunken Greek and Phoenician ships. Vases, jewels. —Fabulous. As we were walking down a nearby street, I spotted a bar where they showed the races on live television. I said, Bilette, suppose we separate just for an hour? Hélène said, if you step inside that bar, I'll go back to Paris like a shot. She snatched the rolled-up *Paris Turf* out of my pocket and started shaking the roll in all directions. —What's the use of being married if we don't do anything together? What's the use? —The Phoenicians bore me, Bilette. —If the Phoenicians bore you, you shouldn't have ruined the tournament for us. —I'm not the one who ruined the tournament. —It wasn't you? It wasn't you who went crazy? It wasn't you who insulted me and vomited? —It was me. But not without cause. We'd inadvertently drifted into the roadway, and a driver blew his horn at us violently. Hélène struck his hood with the racing form. The guy told her off through the window, and she screamed, shut up! I tried to take her arm and pull her back onto the sidewalk, but she prevented me. —You led the deuce of diamonds, Raoul, I thought you had a diamond honor. —If I need you to lead back diamonds, I play the deuce of clubs. —How am I supposed to know you have three clubs to the king? —You don't know it, but when you see me play the nine, you have to think that's a signal. What do you call it, Hélène, when your partner plays a nine? You call it a sig-nal. —I interpreted it wrong. —You didn't interpret it wrong, you don't look at the cards, you stopped looking at the cards years ago. —How do you know, you don't play with me anymore! —And with good reason! A small group had formed around us. Hélène's pink straw hat was too big for her (she'd been right about that), and I felt rather ridiculous with mine. Her eyes were moist and her nose was turning red. I noticed that she must have bought herself some Provençal earrings. I suddenly felt a surge of affection for that little woman, the love of my life, and I said, my Bilette, I'm sorry, I get upset about nothing, come on, let's go to your museum, it'll do me good to see amphorae and stuff like that. While I was leading her away (and directing a little good-bye wave to the onlookers), Hélène said, if the old stones bore you, Rouli, shall we go somewhere else? They don't bore me at all, I said, and watch this. With a solemn gesture, I took the copy of *Paris Turf* away from her and threw it in a trash bin. As we walked along the crowded streets with our arms around each other's waist, I said, and then afterward we'll pass by the casino. It opens at four o'clock. If you don't want to stay with me at the blackjack table, you can go and try your luck at little roulette, my Bilette.

Virginie Déruelle

I heard Édith Piaf howling while I was still on the stairs. I don't know how the other residents tolerate so many decibels. Personally, I don't care one bit for those voices of wretchedness and those rolled, throaty r's. It's like I'm being attacked. My grand-aunt lives in an old folks' home. To be more precise, in a room in an old folks' home, because she almost never leaves it, and if I were her I'd do the same. She makes crocheted patchwork items—quilts, pillowcases, or just squares of no particular use. In fact, nothing my aunt makes is of any particular use, because her productions are ghastly dust traps and old-fashioned to boot. You accept them and pretend to be happy with them, but as soon as you get home you put them way in the back of a closet. Out of superstition, nobody dares throw them away, and you can't find anyone to unload them on. Recently, she was given a CD player that's easy for her to operate. She loves Tino Rossi. But she also listens to Édith Piaf and certain Yves Montand songs. When I enter her room, my grand-aunt's trying to water a cactus and wetting the whole shelf while Piaf bellows, "I'd go to the end of the world, / I'd have my hair curled, / If you asked me to..." I immediately turn down the sound and say, Marie-Paule, the cactus doesn't need very much water. This one's different, my grand-aunt says, this one loves water, was it you who just turned off "Hymne à l'amour"? —I didn't turn it off, I lowered the volume. —How are you, darling? Oh my, don't break your neck wearing those shoes, you're way up there, my goodness. —It's you that's shrinking, Marie-Paule. —Lucky for me I'm shrinking, you see where I live. "My country I'd deny, / I'd tell my friends good-bye, / If you asked me to…" I turn off the music. I say, she gets on my nerves. Who? asks my aunt, Cora Vaucaire? —It's not Cora Vaucaire, Marie-Paule, it's Édith Piaf. —No indeed not, it's Cora Vaucaire. "Hymne à l'amour" is Cora Vaucaire, I still have my wits about me, says my aunt. If you say so, I say, but it's the song that gets on my nerves, I'm against love songs. The more famous they are, the stupider they are. If I were queen of the world, I'd ban them. My aunt shrugs. Who knows what you like, you young people these days? says my aunt. Do you want some orange juice, Virginie? She shows me a bottle that's been open for about a thousand years. I decline it and say, young people these days adore love songs, all the singers sing love songs, it's only me who can't stand them. You'll change your mind the day you meet a boy you like, says my aunt. She's managed to irritate me in thirty seconds. As fast as my mother. It must be a distinguishing trait of the women in my family. On her night table there's a framed photograph of her husband smoking a pipe. One day she showed me the drawer in her dresser that's entirely dedicated to him. She's kept all his letters, his notes, his little gifts. I don't have a clear memory of my granduncle, I was too little when he died. I sit down. I let myself drop into the big, soft armchair that takes up too much space. It's sad, this room. It's got too many things in it, too much furniture. I take the balls of cotton yarn she ordered out of my purse. She hastens to arrange them in a basket at the foot of her bed. Then she sits in the other armchair and says, all right, good, tell me what's going on. When she has all her wits about her, it's hard to understand what she's doing here, alone in this penal colony, far from everything. From time to time, when I call her on the telephone, I have the impression she's just been crying. But ever since the episode of the exploding rice dish, I know my aunt's brain is working less and less, to use her expression. The last time my parents and I were at her house, she'd placed a big glass dish filled with rice left over from the previous evening on a hot griddle two hours before dinner. This warming method left the rice at the top cold. My aunt went into her kitchen to stir the rice with a spatula, that is, to project a lot of it onto her work surface. It was impossible to give her advice or even to enter the room. We caught a glimpse of her through the partly open door, up to her elbows in rice, mixing it with her hands as if she was shampooing a mangy dog. At eight o'clock the dish exploded, strewing the kitchen with grains of rice and shards of glass. After that incident, my parents decided to put her in a home. I say, did you like it when Raymond smoked his pipe? —He smoked a pipe? —In that photo, he's smoking a pipe. —Oh, he gave himself airs from time to time, and besides, I couldn't control everything, you know. When are you going to get married, sweetie? I say, I'm twenty-five, Marie-Paule, I've got a lot of time. She says, do you want some orange juice? —No, thanks. I ask her, were you faithful to each other? She laughs. She raises her eyes to the ceiling and says, a leather goods salesman, what do you think, I couldn't have cared less, you know! With some people, you can't see their youthful face anymore, the years have erased it. With others it's the opposite, when their faces light up they look like kids. I see that at the clinic, even with people who are gravely ill. And my little Marie-Paule is like that too. —Was Raymond talkative? She considers the question and then says, no, not so much, a man doesn't need to be talkative. Right you are, I say. She twists a strand of wool around her fingers and says, my brain's still working, you know. —I know your brain's still working, and that's why I want you to advise me on an important matter. All right, she says. Do you want some orange juice? No, thanks, I say. So here's the thing. Do you remember that I'm a medical secretary? —Yes yes yes, you're a medical secretary. —I work in a clinic with two oncologists. —Yes yes yes. —Well, one of Doctor Chemla's patients, a woman about your age, always comes in accompanied by her son. He must be nice, says my aunt. —He's very nice. Especially since his mother's a pain in the ass. He's old, imagine, he may even be forty. But I like older men. Boys of my age bore me. One day I found myself having a cigarette with him outside. To tell you the truth, I'd noticed him some time before. I'll describe him to you: he's dark-haired, not very tall, he looks like a slightly less handsome version of the actor Joaquin Phoenix, you know who I mean? A Spaniard, says my aunt. —Yes, but...it doesn't matter. Anyway, we're standing under the awning and smoking. I smile at him. He smiles back at me. There we are, smoking and smiling at each other. I try to make my cigarette last, but I finish it before he finishes his. I'm still at work, I've got my white coat on, so there's no reason for me to linger. I say to him, see you soon, and I go back to my basement floor. Time passes, he brings his mother in for several visits, I exchange a few words with him. I make their appointments, I find addresses for his mother's supplementary care. One day she gives me some chocolates and says,

Vincent chose them, and another time I see him waiting for an elevator that doesn't come and I show him where the staff elevator is, you get the picture, that sort of thing. On the days when the name Zawada, their name, is written in the appointment book, I'm happy, I apply my makeup with special care. Do you want a glass of orange juice? my aunt asks. —No, thanks. His name is Vincent Zawada. A lovely name, don't you think? Oh yes, says my aunt. —I'm in heaven at the moment, they show up every week because she's having a course of radiation therapy. So last Monday, there we were again, he and I, smoking under the awning outside. This time he was there first. He's like Raymond. Not at all talkative. My aunt nods. She's listening to me quietly with her hands in her lap, one on top of the other. Every now and then she looks outside. Right in front of the window, two poplars partly block the view of the opposite buildings. I say, so I muster up all my nerve and dare to ask him what he does. It's a little odd, you understand, a man who's always free during the day. My aunt says, true, true. She opens her night-blue eyes very wide. She can thread a little needle without wearing glasses. I say, he's a musician. He tells me he's a pianist and also a composer. Not long after that, he finishes his cigarette. And then, instead of going back to his mother in the waiting room, and without any reason, because neither one of us is talking just then, he stays. He waits for me. He has no reason to remain outside, don't you agree? My aunt shakes her head. It was cold and nasty besides, I say. We stayed outside, both of us, just like the first time, standing there and smiling at each other. I couldn't think of anything to say. Generally I'm pretty fearless, but around that man I feel shy. When I finish my cigarette, he pushes the glass door open to let me go in ahead of him (which proves that he was waiting for me), and he says, let's take your elevator. Each of us could have taken a different elevator, or he could have said nothing, right? Let's take your elevator, that's a way of connecting us, don't you think? I ask. My aunt says, yes, I do. The elevator's very deep, I say, it has to accommodate gurneys, but he stands next to me as if we were in a tiny cabin. I can't say he glued himself to me, I tell my aunt, but I swear to you, Marie-Paule, considering the size of the elevator, he really stood very close. Unfortunately, it's a quick trip from the ground floor to the second level down. After we got out, we walked a few steps together, then he went back to the waiting room and I returned to the secretary's office. Almost nothing happened, that is, nothing specific, but when we separated at the intersection of the corridors, I felt like we were parting on a train platform after a secret trip. Do you think I'm in love, Marie-Paule? Oh yes, my aunt says, you do seem to be. —You know, I've never been in love. Or if I was, it was only for two hours. Two hours, that's not much, says my aunt. —And now what should I do? If I just depend on seeing him at the clinic, things won't move forward at all. Between the patients, the telephone, and the medical consultation reports, I'm simply not free when I'm at the clinic. No, says my aunt. —Do you think he likes me? He likes me, isn't that obvious? Oh, he surely likes you, says my aunt, is he Spanish? Don't trust Spaniards. —But he's not Spanish! —Ah, well, so much the better. My aunt gets up and goes to the window. The two trees outside are moving in the wind. They sway together, and the branches and leaves all do their frenzied dances in the same direction. My aunt says, look at my poplars, look at how much fun they're having. You see where I've been put. Fortunately, I have my two big boys there. They cover my windowsill with their seeds, you know, their little caterpillars, and that makes the birds come. Don't you want some orange juice? No, thanks, Marie-Paule, I say, I have to go. My aunt gets up and starts digging around in her wool basket. She says, can you bring me a ball of Diana-Noel yarn, green, like this one? Of course I can, I say. I give her a big hug. She's minuscule, my Marie-Paule. It breaks my heart to leave her there all alone. On my way down the stairs, I hear Édith Piaf again. She's singing a catchy tune, and it sounds like someone's singing with her. I go back up a few steps, and then I can make out my aunt's thin voice: "It's strange, what a change, / I'm yours in word and deed. / You're the man, you're the man, you're the man that I need."

Rémi Grobe

So I'm supposed to be what? I asked her. —An associate. —An associate? I'm not a lawyer. A journalist, Odile said. —Like your husband? —Why not? —With what newspaper? —Something serious. *Les Échos*. Nobody up there reads that. Later, when we got to Wandermines, Odile wanted me to park the car in a narrow side street behind the church square. But it's raining, I said. —I don't want to arrive in a BMW. —That's the wrong attitude. You'll arrive in the same kind of car the boss's lawyer has, it's perfect. She hesitated. She'd opted for an adorable look, heels higher than usual, power haircut. I said, you're very chic, you're *la Parisienne*, you think they want some left-wing activist type with clogs on her feet showing up to represent them? All right, she said. I believe the main reason she agreed was the rain. I parked on the square and went around the car holding an umbrella. She got out. Small, wrapped in a coat, a scarf tied around her neck, carrying a stiff purse and a briefcase full of folders. I started to have a feeling, I mean a real feeling, at that moment. As we were getting out of the car, in Wandermines, in the rain. The influence of place on our emotions doesn't get its just due. Without warning, certain nostalgias rise to the surface. People change their natures, as in old tales. There in front of the church, which was half hidden in mist, in the square with the red brick buildings and the fried food vendor's shack, I saw the asbestos victims' leading lawyer as a little girl, unsure of herself, who laughed—I adore her laugh—when she recognized the group there to welcome her. Amid that fellowship dressed in Sunday clothes and hastening to the mayor's office to escape the raindrops, as I held Odile's arm to help her cross the slippery square, I felt the catastrophe of sentiment. There had never been any question of that sort of foolishness before. I know her husband, she knows the women who pass in and out of my life. There's never been anything at stake between us except sexual distraction. I said to myself, you're having a fade-out moment, my boy, it will pass. In the municipal hall, Odile spoke before three hundred people, the workers and their families. At the end of her talk, everybody applauded. The president of the victims' association told her, you just filled three buses for the demonstration next Thursday. Odile said in my ear, I was born to be a politician. Her face was beet-red. I nearly told her that politics requires greater composure, but I didn't say anything. We left the general assembly hall for another hall, where a banquet was held. Three o'clock in the afternoon came and we still hadn't made it past the sparkling wine aperitifs. A plump woman of about sixty, wearing a pleated skirt, directed the service. There was a sound system that had been cutting-edge in the 1980s. I struck up an acquaintance with a former worker in asbestos removal and demolition, a guy with pleural cancer. He told me about his working life, about cutting up the corrugated sheets, about grinding or sanding pipes with sandpaper and no protection. He described the asbestos room, the dust. He told me the asbestos was delivered to them in drums and they'd play with it like snow. I saw Odile dancing the Madison with several widows (she's the one who said *Madison*, I know nothing about dances) and a kind of tango with some men strapped to oxygen tanks. A woman called out, Odile, your hair looks like you used a rake on it, you need to get yourself a permanent! I thought, this is real life, tables on trestles, fraternity, dust, Odile Toscano dancing in a village hall. I thought, that's what you should have done in life, Rémi, you should have been mayor of Wandermines in the Nord-Pas-de-Calais, with its church, its factory, its cemetery. The servers brought out coq au vin in big cooking pots. My new pal told me that the number of recent graves in the cemetery was higher than the population of the village. We're fighting, he said. I thought about the force of that word. He said, when my brother died, I had "Le Temps des cerises" sung at his funeral. My head was about to explode. When the end of the day finally came, I got behind the wheel to drive to Douai, but I was as loaded as Odile. Once we were in the hotel room, she collapsed on the bed. She said, I'm sloshed, Rémi, I can't very well call the children in this state, do you have some aspirin? —I have something better. I took a bottle of cognac from the minibar. I was sloshed too, and the bewilderment I felt persisted. The way she was lying there, the way she pulled a pillow under her head, the way she knocked back the shot of cognac. Her laugh, her weary face. I thought, she's mine, my little Counselor Toscano. I lay on top of her, kissed her, undressed her. We made love with incipient hangovers, which added just the right dose of pain. Around ten in the evening, we got hungry. The hotel clerk told us about a restaurant that would still be open. Before we found it, we wandered around Douai. We walked along a river called the Scarpe, Odile told me, I don't know why I remember that name. She told me other things about some of the buildings and showed me the law courts. It was pretty windy and drizzly, but I liked the opaque temperament of the place, the silence, the amusing streetlights, I was ready to stay and live there. Odile trod along bravely, her nose swollen by the cold. I had an urge to wrap my arms around her, to hold her close against me, but I restrained myself. There had never been any question of that sort of foolishness between us before. In the restaurant we ordered vegetable soup and ham on the bone. Odile wanted tea, I wanted a beer. She said, you shouldn't drink any more alcohol. I said, it's nice of you to look after me. She smiled. Those people impressed me, I said. I live a stupid fucking life. All the people I know are stupid, stupid and insipid. She said, not everybody's lucky enough to be born in coal-mining country. —You too, you impress me too. Ah, at last! Odile said, making a gesture that meant I should develop this line of thought. —You're involved, engaged, strong. You're beautiful. —Rémi? Hello? Are you all right? —Don't, I'm serious. You fight with them, for them. —That's my job. —You could do it differently. You could be more aloof. The workers love you. Odile laughed (I've already mentioned that I adore her laugh). —The workers love me! The common people love me, you see, I really should go into politics. And you, my poor darling, you're going to sleep well tonight. —You're wrong to laugh. I'm serious. The way you danced and cleared away the plates, the comforting words you said, you made the day enchanting. —You didn't think those pants made me look fat? —No. —You think my hair looks like I used a rake on it? —Yes, but I like it better than the helmet look you had this morning. And suddenly I thought, tomorrow we'll be in Paris.

Tomorrow evening, Odile will be at home in her cozy cell, with husband and children. And me, I'll be the devil knows where. Ordinarily none of that mattered, but since things had taken an abnormal turn, I thought, take your precautions, old boy. I pulled my cell phone out of my pocket, said excuse me to Odile, and looked for Loula Moreno's number. She's beautiful, she's funny, she's desperate. Exactly what I need. I sent her a text message: "Free tomorrow evening?" Odile was blowing on her soup. I felt myself invaded by a kind of panic. A dread of abandonment. When I was a child, my parents would leave me with other people. I'd find a dark spot and remain there immobile, getting smaller and smaller. The screen on my cell phone lit up and I read, "Free tomorrow evening, my angel, but you'll have to come to Klosterneuburg." I remembered that Loula was making a movie in Austria. Let's see, who else... Everything OK? Odile asked. Everything's fine, I said. —You look frustrated. —A client postponing a meeting, nothing important. And then I put on an indifferent air and tossed out, what are you doing tomorrow evening? We're celebrating my mother's seventieth birthday, Odile replied. —At your place? —No, at my parents' house in Boulogne. Having guests is good for my mother. Doing the shopping, cooking for everybody. I have a fear of my parents sitting around being depressed. —Don't they do anything? —My father was a senior inspector of finances. When Raymond Barre was prime minister, my father was one of his advisers, and later he was director of the Wurmster Bank. Ernest Blot, ever heard of him? —Vaguely. —He had to retire from the bank because of a heart problem. Now he's chairman of the board of directors, but it's just an honorary position. He does a little volunteer work, he spins his wheels.

My mother does nothing. She feels alone. My father's hateful to her, they should have separated a long time ago. Odile fished the slice of lemon out of her empty teacup and separated the peel from the pulp. One of the effects of emotional malfunction is that nothing gets passed over anymore. Everything stands for something else, everything's in code and needs deciphering. I was unhinged enough to imagine that Odile's last words contained a message, and so I asked her, have you ever thought about separating, you and your husband? I immediately covered her face with my hands and said, I don't give a damn, forget I said that, I absolutely don't give a damn. When I removed my hands, Odile said, he must think about it every day, I'm horrible. I'm sure you are, I said. Robert's horrible too, but he knows how to make it up with me, Odile said, swallowing the lemon slice. I didn't like that she'd chosen the same meaningless adjective for both of them, and I didn't like that she'd said the name Robert, that Robert had barged into our conversation. That she could offer such a banal glimpse into their life together, about which I could not have cared less, irritated me. It's foolish to think that sentiment brings us closer. It does the opposite, it sanctifies the distances between people. In the excitement of the day, in the rain, on the platform with a microphone in her hand, in the car, in the room with the curtains drawn, Odile felt near, her face in reach of my hand, of my kisses. But in that gloomy, virtually empty restaurant where I'd begun, against my will, to scrutinize her smallest gesture and the tone of her every word with feverish attention, she'd ducked away from me, she'd vanished into a world I had no part in. I said, if I had to live here, at the end of two days I'd blow my brains out. Odile laughed (I found her laugh caustic and conventional). —You claimed the opposite ten minutes ago. You were enthusiastic about Douai. —I've changed my mind. I'd blow my brains out. She shrugged and dunked a bit of bread in the remains of her soup. I had the feeling she was on the verge of boredom. I was on the verge of boredom myself, permeated with the sullenness of lovers when nothing's going on outside the bed. I couldn't think of anything to say. I heard the rain return and start pattering against the window. Odile put on a look of consternation and said, we didn't take the umbrella. I thought about the asbestos demolition worker who showed his thoroughly stained teeth when he laughed, about the chubby organizer in the pleated skirt that made her look even fatter, and God knows why, about my father, an auto body mechanic whose shop was on the Avenue de la Porte de Pantin, on the edge of Paris, and who used to complain bitterly about whoever had installed the leaky skylight. I was tempted to tell Odile that story, but the temptation lasted half a second. I scrolled through the list of contacts on my cell phone and came upon Yorgos Katos. I thought, there you go, my boy, you can sally forth and lose your shirt at poker. I texted Yorgos: "Need an easy mark at the table tomorrow night?" Odile asked, who are you writing to? —Yorgos Katos. Haven't I ever spoken to you about Yorgos? —Never. —He's a friend who makes his living gambling. One day, years ago, he was playing with Omar Sharif in a bridge tournament. He could feel a crowd of girls gathered at his back. He told himself, they know I play much better than he does. It never occurred to him for a second that they wanted to see Omar Sharif's face. Odile said she was in love with the desert prince in *Lawrence of Arabia*. As far as she was concerned, Omar Sharif wore a keffiyeh and rode a black charger, he didn't sit huddled at a bridge table. I realized she was absolutely right. I felt lighthearted again. Everything returned to normal.

Chantal Audouin

A man's a man. There are no married men, no men who are off limits. None of that exists (as I explained to Doctor Lorrain the day I was committed). When you meet someone, you're not interested in his marital status. Or his sentimental condition. Sentiments are mutable and mortal. Like every earthly thing. Animals die. So do plants. Watercourses aren't the same from one year to the next. Nothing lasts. People want to believe the opposite. They spend their lives gluing pieces back together, and they call that marriage or fidelity or whatever. As for me, I don't burden myself with such idiocy anymore. I try my luck with whomever I like. I'm not afraid of coming up short. And in any case, I've got nothing to lose. I won't be beautiful forever. My mirror's already growing less and less friendly. One day Jacques Ecoupaud's wife—Jacques Ecoupaud, the minister, my lover—one day his wife called and suggested we meet. I was stunned. She must have been nosing around in his computer, and she'd come across some e-mail exchanges between Jacques and me. At the end of the conversation, before hanging up, she said, I hope you won't tell him anything about this, I'd like it to remain strictly between us. I called up Jacques immediately and said, I'm seeing your wife this Wednesday. Jacques seemed to know all about it. He sighed. It was a coward's sigh, and its meaning was, well, since there's no way around it. Couples disgust me. Their hypocrisy. Their smugness. To this day I've been unable to do anything to resist the attraction exerted upon me by Jacques Ecoupaud. A lady-killer. My male counterpart. Except that he's a junior government minister, a secretary of state (but he always says *minister*). With all the appurtenances. Cars with tinted windows, chauffeur, bodyguard. A restaurant table always set aside for him. Me, I started from less than scratch. I don't even have a high school diploma. I climbed up the slope without anyone's help. These days I'm in event decoration. I've made a little name for myself, I work in the film world, in politics. Once I dressed a function room in Bercy where a National Seminar on the Performance of Self-Employed French Entrepreneurs was being held (I can still remember its title; we stuck flags into the flower bouquets). That was the event where I met Jacques. The Secretary of State for Tourism and the Craft Industry. A pathetic title, if you consider it closely. The kind of no-necked, stocky man who steps into a room and scans it to make sure he's caught everyone's eye. The hall was packed with entrepreneurs from the provinces who'd come to Paris like visiting nobility, accompanied by their dressed-to-the-nines wives. During the event, a vice-president of a chamber of trades made a speech. I was at the back of the hall, near a window, and Jacques Ecoupaud came up to me and said, you see the guy who just started talking? Yes, I said. —You see his bow tie? —Yes. —It's a bit large, don't you think? Yes, it is, I said. It's made of wood, said Jacques Ecoupaud. —Wood? The boy's a craftsman, a framing carpenter, Jacques said. He made a bow tie out of wood and shined it up with Pledge. I laughed and Jacques laughed, with his laugh that's half seduction and half electoral campaign. And you see the one with the velvet James Bond briefcase?

Jacques asked. Do you know what his name is? It's Frank Ravioli. And he sells dry dog food. The following day Jacques parked his Citroën C5 outside my apartment building and we spent the first part of the night together. Usually, where men are involved, I'm the one who leads the dance. I turn them on, I wrap them up, and I clear out just at daybreak. Sometimes I let myself go with the flow. I get a little attached. It lasts while it lasts. As long as I'm not bored. Jacques Ecoupaud pulled the rug out from under me. To this day I cannot understand what it was that made me so utterly dependent on that man. A no-neck guy who comes up to my shoulder. A standard-issue sweet-talker. He immediately presented himself as a great libertine. Like, I'm going to corrupt you, little girl, that sort of thing. He always called me little girl. I'm fifty-six years old and five feet ten inches tall, with an Anita Ekberg–type chest. Being called little girl moved me. It's stupid. A great libertine, and you can say it again. I still don't know what it means. As for me, I was ready to experience things. One evening he came to my house with a woman. A brunette around forty who worked in public housing. Her name was Corinne. I served aperitifs. Jacques took off his coat and tie and sprawled on the sofa. The woman and I stayed in our armchairs and talked about the weather and the neighborhood. Jacques said, make yourselves comfortable, my dears. We undressed a little, but not completely. Corinne seemed accustomed to that kind of situation. The girl with no emotions who does what she's told. She took off her brassiere and hung it on a potted chrysanthemum. Jacques laughed. We were both wearing the same type of lingerie, designed to arouse a dead man. At a certain point, Jacques spread out his arms symmetrically and said,

come here, both of you! We each sat on one side of him, and
he closed his arms around us. We stayed like that for a while,
giggling, stroking his big hairy belly, tickling his fly, and then
all at once he said, come on, girls, get closer! That sentence
still makes me feel ashamed. Ashamed of our position, of the
bright light, of the way Jacques was completely lacking in
imagination and dominance. I'd been expecting the Marquis
de Sade, and I found myself with a flabby fellow who wal-
lowed on my sofa and said, *come on, girls, get closer.* But in
those days, I let everything pass. If men wanted to acknowl-
edge a single quality in us, that would be the one. We reha-
bilitate them. We lift them up as soon as we can. We don't
want to know that the driver is a former customs officer, that
the bodyguard is a yokel from the South who used to work
in security for the department of Cantal. That the Citroën
C5 is the worst of all fleet vehicles. That the great libertine
had set out to corrupt us without even bringing along a
bottle of champagne. Thérèse Ecoupaud—Jacques's wife—
arranged to meet me in a café near the Trinity church. She
told me, I'll be wearing a beige jacket and reading *Le Monde.*
A fun prospect. I planned to get a manicure and to have my
hair dyed the day before our date. The hairdresser made me
an even more golden blonde than usual. I spent an hour
choosing my outfit. I opted for a red skirt and a green crew-
necked sweater. A pair of high-heeled Gigi Dool shoes. And
to make the most of my arrival, a little putty-colored
English-style trench coat. She was already there. I spotted her
at once. Through the window, from the street. Probably my
age, but looking ten years older. Slapdash makeup. Short,
badly cut hair with visible roots. Blue scarf over a loose beige
jacket. I thought right there, it's over. Jacques Ecoupaud,

that's all over. I almost didn't go into the café. The sight of the legitimate, neglected wife was much more lethal than all the disappointments, the waiting, the broken promises, the plates and candles set out for nobody. Her table was practically on the terrace, in full view. She had her spectacles perched on the end of her nose, and she was absorbed in reading her newspaper. Like a Latin professor waiting for her student. In her preparations to meet her husband's mistress, Thérèse Ecoupaud hadn't paid the slightest attention to her appearance. What man can live with a woman like that? Couples disgust me. Their reciprocal wizening, their dusty connivance. I don't like anything about that ambulant structure, or about the way it cruises through time taunting those who are alone. Nevertheless, I went to the café. I extended my hand. I said, Chantal Audouin. She said, Thérèse Ecoupaud. I ordered a Bellini to get on her nerves. I unbuttoned my coat but didn't take it off, like a woman who has only a little time to dedicate to the present obligation. She let me know immediately that she felt nothing but indifference. I hardly got a look from her. She was intent on rolling her coffee spoon between her thumb and index finger. She said, Madame, my husband sends you e-mails. You answer him. He makes declarations to you. You incite him. When you get upset, he apologizes. He consoles you. You forgive him. Et cetera. The problem with this correspondence, Madame, is that you think it unique. You've constructed an imaginary tableau, where on one side there's you, the warrior's safe haven of repose, and on the other his tiresome wife and his public service career. You've never imagined that he could be maintaining other liaisons at the same time. You've thought you were the only woman in whom my husband confides, the only one to whom he would send, for example, a message at two a.m., referring to himself as Jacquot (but I won't dwell on such foolishness): "Poor Jacquot, alone in his room in Montauban, missing your skin, your lips, and your...," you know the rest. The same text for each of his three recipients. That night, there were three of you who received that message. You were more eager than the others, you replied with great warmth and, how shall I say it, innocence. I wanted to meet you because it seemed to me that you were particularly enamored of my husband, Thérèse Ecoupaud continued. I guessed that you'd be happy to receive this information about him so that you could avoid falling from too great a height, the horrible woman said. I asked Doctor Lorrain, I said, doesn't it seem normal to you, Doctor, that a person would try to kill herself after such a scene? Of course, the best solution would have been to kill the man. I applaud women who slaughter their lovers, but not everybody has the right temperament for that. Doctor Lorrain asked me how I felt about Jacques Ecoupaud now that I was getting better. I said, he's a sorry little man. Doctor Lorrain raised his arms in his white coat and repeated my words, as if I'd just found the key to independence: a sorry little man! —Yes, Doctor, a sorry little man. But as you see, sorry little men can still fool idiots. And how does it help me now to see him as a sorry little man? The thought of that sorry little man degrades me, it does me no good at all. What makes you think confronting reality soothes the heart? Igor Lorrain nodded like a man showing that he understands everything and wrote I don't know what assessment in my folder. After I left his office, I ran into one of his other patients, my favorite, on the stairs of the clinic. He's a long-limbed, brown-haired young man with beautiful bright eyes, always smiling. A Québécois. He said, hello Chantal. I said, hello Céline. I'd told him my name was Chantal, and he'd said his was Céline. I think he believes he's Céline Dion, the singer. But maybe he's joking. He's always got a scarf wrapped around his neck. I see him roaming the corridors or, when the weather's good, strolling along the alleys in the garden. He moves his lips and says words you can't quite hear. He doesn't look straight at people. It's as though he's addressing a distant fleet, as though he's praying on top of a rock, hoping to attract the ships he spies far out at sea, like someone in a mythic tale.

Jean Ehrenfried

Darius sat in the huge orthopedic chair, in which, if you ask me, no one can be comfortable. He sat down and slumped against the back of the chair like a defeated man. If anyone had come into the room just then, they wouldn't have been able to tell which of us—Darius, collapsed in the chair, or me, lying bandaged in the bed and hooked up to a drip—was the more pitiful. I waited for him to speak. He sat there for a while, and then, with his neck thrust forward by the sausage-shaped headrest, he said, Anita has left me. Even though I was reclining on my hospital bed, I found myself looking down at him. The fact that he'd been able to pronounce those words with that crestfallen look on his face struck me as verging on comical. And all the more so when he added, in a barely audible voice, she left with the landscaper. —The landscaper? —Yes, the guy who's been designing that shitty garden in Gassin for the past three years, who's making me spend a fortune on scary sub-Saharan plants. I first met Darius long before he was kicked out of the Third Circle, one of those exclusive clubs where oligarchs from both right and left connive together, steeped in right-mindedness and filled with devoted allegiance to the power of money. At the time I met him, he was the director of several companies, one of them a team of engineering consultants and another that manufactured smart cards, if memory serves. As for me, I had just left the international division of Safranz-Ulm

Electric to take over as chairman of its board of directors. I was filled with affection for that young man, nearly twenty-five years my junior, and his Oriental charm. He was married to Anita, the daughter of a British lord, with whom he had two children, both of them more or less messed up. Darius Ardashir was as cunning as could be. He slithered into the system with disarming nonchalance, showing great aptitude for the mutual boosting, the favor-swapping, the manipulation of pawns in high places. He was never in a hurry, his feelings never hurt. The same way with women. Eventually he made a fortune as an intermediary in some international contracts. He got entangled in various cases of corruption, the thorniest of which concerned the sale of a border surveillance system to Nigeria, which incidentally led to his ouster from the Third Circle (the way I see it, a club that expels its rogues is a fucked-up club). Some of his connections did a bit of time in prison, but he himself escaped without any real damage. I've always found him a resilient man and a faithful friend. When I was attacked by this blasted cancer, Darius behaved like a son. Before engaging in a serious conversation with him, I pressed all sorts of buttons in an effort to raise the head of my bed. Darius contemplated my efforts and the succession of preposterous positions they resulted in with dull eyes and without moving. A nurse came in—I'd no doubt rung for her—and said, Monsieur Ehrenfried, what are you trying to do? —Sit up! —Doctor Chemla will be dropping in. He knows you're not running a fever anymore. —Tell him I'm fed up and I want him to let me leave. She tidied my bed and tucked me in like a child. I asked Darius if he wanted something to drink. He declined, and the girl left the room. I said, all right, this landscaper, isn't he simply a moment of passing madness? —She wants a divorce. I let a minute or so pass and then said, you've never paid much attention to Anita. He gave me an astonished look, as if I'd uttered some insanity. —She had the best life in the world. I understand, I said. —I gave her everything. Name one thing she didn't have. Houses, jewelry, servants. Extravagant trips. She won't get anything, Jean. All my assets are in my companies. The villa in Gassin, the house on Rue de la Tour, the furniture, the art, nothing's in my name. Those two can die for all I care. —You cheated on her day and night. —What does that have to do with anything? —You can't begrudge her taking a lover. —Women don't take lovers. They get infatuated, they make it into a big drama, they go completely crazy. A man needs a safe place to go to so he can face the world. You can't deploy if you don't have a fixed point, a base camp. Anita's the house. She's the family. If you want a breath of fresh air, it doesn't mean you don't want to go home. I don't get attached to women. The only one that counts is the next one. But that stupid bitch goes to bed with the gardener and wants to run off with him. What sense does that make? While listening to Darius, I was watching my IV drip. The drops looked strangely irregular, and I was on the verge of calling the nurse. I said, would you have accepted it if she lived the way you do? —What does that mean? —If she had insignificant affairs. He shook his head. Then he reached into a pocket, extracted a white handkerchief, and folded it carefully before blowing his nose. I thought, that gesture's the exclusive property of this particular type of man. He said, no, because that's not her style. Then, in a mournful voice, he added, I was in London the past two days—an important trip, which she totally wrecked for me—and on the way back, the TGV stopped a few minutes north of the French border, in some outlying area. Right in front of my window there was a little detached house, red brick, red roof tiles, well-maintained wooden fence. Geraniums in the windows. And more flowers in hanging pots on the walls. You know what I thought, Jean? I thought, in that house, someone has decided you have to be happy. I thought he was going to continue, but he fell silent. He was staring at the floor with a face full of gloom. I said to myself, he's at the end of his rope. If a Darius Ardashir starts finding evidence of happiness in brickwork and macramé, that's the hallmark of total dejection. Or a simpler sign, I thought, and a more troubling one as far as he was concerned, was the mere fact that he could refer to happiness as an end in itself. As for me, I thought I should summon the emergency medical staff, because the IV tube was carrying air bubbles to my arm. Do you know how old Anita is? Darius asked. —Are those bubbles normal? —What bubbles? Those are drops. It's the product. —Do you think so? Look closer. He took out his glasses and got up to observe the tube. —They're drops. —Are you sure? Tap the bag. —What for? —Just tap it, tap it. It helps. Darius tapped the bag of intravenous fluid a few times and sat back down. I said, I can't see anything anymore. I'm sick of being hooked up to all this plumbing. —Do you know how old Anita is? —Tell me. —Forty-nine years old. You think that's the age to develop blossoming ambitions, romantic passions, and other nonsense? You know, I often think about Dina, Jean. You had a wife who understood life. Dina's in heaven. You all don't have Paradise, do you? Jews? What do you have? —We don't have anything. —Well, she's surely in a good place. She left you your sons, very nice boys who take care of you, and your daughter too, your son-in-law, your grandchildren. Dina knew how to create an environment. When you're old, having a hand to grab on to is important. Me, I'm going to end up like a rat. Anita will tell you I got what I deserved. Another idiotic phrase. What does whatever I deserve have to do with any of this? I have a magnificent apartment, magnificent properties, what do people think, do they think all that just falls out of the sky? It happens because I'm killing myself, I leave at eight in the morning, I go to bed at midnight, and she doesn't understand that I do it for her? And the boys—a pair of zeros who are going to squander everything—they don't understand it's for them? No, they don't. They complain, complain, complain. And have a fling with a moron who plants frangipani. I would've liked it better if she'd run off with a woman. I asked him, are you all right in that chair? —I'm just fine. The previous evening, Ernest sat there for less than a minute before opting for the folding chair. While I listened to Darius, I remembered an afternoon of tidying up that Dina and I had spent at home. We found some old-fashioned linens, hand-embroidered, passed down from her mother, and a lovely Italian dinner service. We said to each other, what's the use of all this now? Dina spread out a well-ironed, yellowing tablecloth on a sofa. She lined up the inlaid porcelain cups. As time passes, objects that once had value become useless burdens. I didn't know what to say to Darius. The couple is the most impenetrable thing there is. You can't understand a couple, even if you're part of it. Doctor Chemla came into the room. As smiling and congenial as always. I was glad he'd come, because I was getting gangrene in my arm. I introduced them: Darius Ardashir, a dear friend,

Doctor Philip Chemla, my savior. And I immediately added, Doctor, don't you think my arm is swollen? If you ask me, the fluid's missing the vein. Chemla palpated my fingers and my forearm. He looked at my wrist, turned the thumb wheel that regulated the IV flow, and said, we'll finish this bag and that'll be it. You'll be home tomorrow. I'll come back and see you this evening, we'll take a little walk in the corridor. After he left, Darius asked, what exactly did you have? —A urinary infection. —How old is he, this doc of yours? —Thirty-six. —Too young. —He's a genius. —Too young. I said, so what are you going to do? He bent forward, spread his arms like a guy lifting the void, and let them drop back down. I saw his eyes wander over my night table, and he said, what are you reading? —*The Destruction of the European Jews*, by Raul Hilberg. —That's all you could find for the hospital? —It's perfect for the hospital. When things aren't going right, you have to read sad books. Darius picked up the thick volume. He flipped through it dull-eyed. —So you recommend this? —Heartily. He managed a smile. Then he put the book down and said, she should have warned me. I can't accept that she cheated on me in secret. Despite Chemla's inspection, I still had the feeling that my arm was swelling up. I said, look at my arms, do you think they're the same size? Darius got up, put his glasses on again, looked at my arms, and said, exactly the same. Then he sat back down. We remained in silence for a brief while, listening to the noises in the corridor, the gurneys, the voices. Then Darius said, women have swiped the martyr's role for themselves. They've theorized about it out loud. They groan and make people feel sorry for them. Whereas in reality, the real martyr is the man. When I heard that, I thought about something my friend Serge said right at the beginning of his struggle with Alzheimer's. For some unknown reason, he wanted to go to Married Man Street. No one knew where Married Man Street was. Eventually, it dawned on his friends that he was talking about Martyrs' Street. I related this story to Darius, who knew Serge distantly. He asked me, how's he doing now? I said, as well as can be expected. The main thing is not to contradict him. I always tell him he's right. Darius nodded. He looked at a point on the floor near the door and said, what a marvelous disease.

Damien Barnèche

My father used to tell me, if anyone asks you what your
father does, say he's a technical consultant. In actual fact, he
used to receive a paycheck as a technical consultant in
exchange for partnering at bridge with a guy who managed
concession agreements. My grandfather bankrupted himself
at the races, and for several years my father was banned from
the gambling casinos. Loula listens to me while I tell her
incredible stories. She's really pretty. She gets into my car
every morning, that is, into the car the movie production
company provides to pick her up and bring her back. She
sits in the front beside me, still a little drowsy. I have orders
not to speak to her unless she addresses me, I'm supposed to
respect her concentration and her exhaustion. But Loula
Moreno asks me questions, she takes an interest in me, she
doesn't talk only about herself the way actresses generally
do. I tell her I like movies, I work in production, but I'd prefer to be involved on the creative side. To tell the truth, I
don't have a very good idea of what I want to do. I'm the
first Barnèche who's not a gambler. Loula uses *tu* when she
talks to me and I reply with *vous*, even though I'm twenty-
two and she's just barely thirty (she told me so). As the days
pass, I tell her my life story. Loula Moreno is curious and
observant. She was quick to notice that I'm interested in
Géraldine, the assistant dresser, a little brunette with bright
eyes and masses of hair. My first impression of this girl was

mixed, because we were talking about music and she revealed right away that she liked the Black-Eyed Peas and Zaz. Normally that would have stopped me in my tracks. But the fact that we were in Klosterneuburg—filming had begun in Austria—may have made me more tolerant (or lamer). Especially as we very quickly discovered a mutual passion for Pim's. We remembered that when we were little, they used to make a white chocolate/cherry Pim's, and we found ourselves agreeing that Casino's later version wasn't as good. Géraldine asked me if I thought Pim's would make a Pim's caramel someday. I said yes, but on the condition that they make the biscuit harder or the liquid caramel very light, because it wouldn't work with soft on soft. Géraldine said, but then it wouldn't be a Pim's anymore. I agreed completely. She'd never tasted Pim's pear, which are quite rare and little known. I told her, the pear is Pim's best product. The jam's relatively thick, unlike the raspberry or orange jam, but you don't notice that except for the moment you bite into it. Then it thins and spreads. The orange cookie gives itself up immediately, the pear takes its time. It melts into the biscuit. Even the wrapper is perfect, the packaging's very chic. They haven't made it some tacky green color, you see, the color they've chosen has some taupe in it. Géraldine was enthused. In the end I said, when you have your first Pim's pear, you've got to look at the package while you eat it. She said, yes, yes, of course! I fell in love with her because it's very rare to find a girl who understands that sort of thing. Loula approves. I can't figure out whether I have a chance with Géraldine. When a girl really attracts me, I'm not the type that goes charging in blindly. I need a guarantee. In Klosterneuburg, I had the impression that she liked me. But ever since we came back, she's been selling herself to the sound assistant. A giant prawn who greets you with the Boy Scout salute (I'm not sure whether he means it or if it's a joke; if it's a joke, it's even worse). And another difficulty, one that didn't exist in Austria, has arisen: she wears ballet shoes. Even with a dress. In college, if you leaned forward you could see a whole forest of legs ending in ballet shoes. To me, ballet shoes are a synonym for boredom and the absence of sex. Loula asked me to make a list of the things I find irritating in girls. I said such a list would extend beyond infinity. —Give it a try. I said, when a girl has a dumb hairdo. When she analyzes everything. When she's religious. When she's a political activist. When all her friends are girls. When she likes Justin Timberlake. When she has a blog. Loula laughed. I said, when she can't laugh like you. One evening, there was a little party for one of the actors who had finished his last day on the shoot. Loula advised me not to let the sound assistant have the field to himself. I wound up sitting shoulder to shoulder with Géraldine at the bottom of the stairs to the basement where the sets are stored. I'd swiped a bottle of red wine, and we were drinking it from plastic cups. Especially me. I said (in the murmuring voice American TV actors use in pre-screw sequences), if I were president, there are a certain number of reforms I'd institute immediately. A European directive against hangers that are supposed to hold your trousers suspended but let them fall as soon as you turn your back. A law against tissue paper in socks (it's called tissue paper, but it's halfway between tissue paper and tracing paper), which is only there to make you waste time and to say to you, I'm new. A law that would protect you from being bothered by the leaflet when trying to open a box of medication. You're groping around for your sleeping pill, your fingers close on paper, and you immediately throw the leaflet away because it's such a pain in the ass. The pharmaceutical companies ought to be indicted for murder, given the risks they force you to run. Géraldine said, you take sleeping pills? —No, antihistamines. —What are they? I wasn't so hammered that I couldn't see the enormity of the problem. Not only was Géraldine not gradually collapsing against my body, charmed by the idiocies I was spouting, she also didn't know the word *antihistamine*. And there was, furthermore, her disapproving tone regarding sleeping pills, a tone that betrayed a rigid personality and new age tendencies. I said, allergy medicine. —You have allergies? —Asthma. —Asthma? What was her problem, why did she repeat everything like that? I took a swig straight from the bottle, put on a doleful voice, and said, and hay fever, and other kinds of allergies. And then I kissed her. She let me. I tipped her over onto the stairs, against the wall of the warehouse, and began feeling her up all over. She wriggled and said something I didn't understand, and that irritated me. I said, what, rubbing myself against her the whole time, what? What did you say? She repeated it, she said, not here, not here, Damien! She tried to push me away the way girls do, half yes, half no, I stuck my head under her T-shirt, she wasn't wearing a bra, I caught a nipple between my lips, I heard incomprehensible moans, I stroked her thighs, her buttocks, I slid my fingers under her panties, I tried to guide her hand to my cock, and all of a sudden she totally arched her back, she thrust me away with her arms, her legs, kicking in all directions and crying out, stop, stop! I found myself flattened against the opposite wall, and in front of me there was a red-faced, infuriated girl. She said, you're crazy! I said, what did I do? —Are you kidding? —I'm sorry, I thought you…you didn't seem to have anything against… —Not here. Not like that. —What does that mean, not like that? —Not so brutally, she said. Not without preliminaries. A woman needs preliminaries, nobody ever taught you that? She tried to fix her hair, she repeated the same gesture ten times in an effort to gather all the strands behind her head. I thought, *preliminaries*, what a dreadful word. I said, leave your hair alone, it looks good when it's a mess. —Messy hair is exactly what I don't want. I drained the bottle to the dregs and said, disgusting rotgut. —Then why are you drinking it? —Come kiss me. —No. They'd put on some music upstairs, but I couldn't make out what it was. I put out a hand like a beggar and said, come on. —No. She fixed her hair in a chignon and stood up. I lay sprawled, my head pressed against the wall. Nothing was happening, absolutely nothing. She stood there before me, her arms dangling at her sides. I slouched on the steps, crushing the plastic cup in one hand. So that was what it was to be young, to have years ahead of you. In other words, nothing. A deep abyss. But not an abyss you fall into. It's above you, in front of you. My father was right to live in a world of cards. Géraldine crouched down next to me. I was starting to get a headache. She asked, are you all right? —Yes. —What are you thinking about? —Nothing. —Yes you are. Tell me. —Nothing, believe me. I waited until I calmed down a little and kissed her without touching anything else. I stood up, straightened my clothes, and said, I'm going back up. She got up at once. I'm going back up too, she said, are you mad? —No. They were getting on my nerves, those equivocations of hers. That soppy voice she had all of a sudden. I climbed the stairs two at a time, I could sense her hurrying to keep up with me. Just before we got to the top, she said, Damien? —What? —Nothing. Up on the ground floor, the party was in full swing, people were dancing. Loula Moreno, of course, had already left. The following day, in the car, I gave her a general description of the evening. Loula asked, how did you part? —I took the car and went home. —How did you say good-bye? —See you, see you, a peck on the cheek. Zero, Loula said. Zero, I repeated. The sun was barely up, the weather was crappy. I'd turned on everything you can turn on in a car, windshield wipers, defogger, defroster, multidirectional heat. I said, in real life I have a scooter. Loula nodded. —I was on roller skates when my friends were riding bicycles, on a bicycle when they had scooters, and now on a scooter when they're driving cars. I'm a boy who knows how to keep in step. I said, there's a very well-known method for getting women, everybody knows it, it's not to say a word. The guys girls like are silent types who make faces. Me, I don't think I'm good-looking enough or intriguing enough to keep quiet. I talk too much, I babble incoherently, I want to be funny all the time. Even with you, I want to be funny. A lot of times, after a barrage of jokes and nonsense, I get gloomy and angry at myself. Especially when they fall flat, I hunker down, I become sinister for fifteen minutes or so. Then I'm my old jolly self again. The whole seduction song-and-dance is a pain in the ass. Loula asked, what kind of scooter do you have? —A Yamaha Xenter 125. Do you know a lot about scooters? —For a while I had a Vespa. Pink, like the one in *Roman Holiday*. I said, I can just picture you. You must have been really cute. Wasn't that movie in black and white? She reflected and then said, ah, yes, it's true, it was. But the scooter seemed pink. Maybe it wasn't pink, after all.

Luc Condamine

Yesterday I whipped Juliette with the dog's leash, I said. Lionel said, you have a dog? Robert was in his kitchen, making a spaghetti dish for us with a Neapolitan sauce. That's the way I prefer to see them, my two jackass friends. Sitting around a kitchen table. Without the women. On our own and at our worst, *dixit* Lionel. I beat my daughter with the dog's leash, I repeated. After an argument caused by her insolence, just as she was leaving the room I said, and don't slam the door! She slammed it all the harder. I picked up the leash, which was lying around somewhere, caught her in the hall, and gave her a thrashing. I didn't feel at all sorry or embarrassed, but rather a sort of relief. That child carries on a reign of terror in the house, she screams at us in this incredibly shrill voice. When Anne-Laure found out I'd whipped our daughter with the dog's leash, she went mute and her features got all distorted. She makes faces like a character in the Yiddish theater to signify her contempt. It's something new. Then she left the room and came back a few minutes later, resolutely silent in that punitive way women have, to display the cuts on the arm and back. I said, serves her right. Juliette, her face all red and swollen, looked me up and down and said, I hate you. I thought she looked cute, and she spoke in a normal tone of voice. Anne-Laure said to me, you ought to see someone. Do you think I need to see someone? I asked. Lionel said, I didn't remember you had a dog. —Actually a long rat. Call that a dog. This wine is really good. Brunello di Montalcino 2006, excellent. I've got no more patience with women. The other day I had my mother talking on the telephone, Anne-Laure in front of the mirror finding wrinkles, and Juliette yelling at her sister, and I said to myself, what the fuck? I'm going to ask the paper to send me somewhere far away. How about Paola? Robert asked, do you still see her? —Yes. But I'm going to stop. You haven't said anything to Odile, have you? —No, no. Why are you going to stop? —Because there comes a moment when the conventional woman starts to show through the courtesan. The only girls I like are the kind that go to sailors' bars, and yet I somehow wind up captivating semi-intellectuals who invite me to poetic evenings. She's worth a lot more than you are, Robert said. —The very thing I have against her. And by the way, what's with Virginie Déruelle? Anything happening there? Who's she? Lionel asked. A little thing he met at his gym and wants to pass on to me, Robert said. —And passed on to you. —Whatever. —Fine, so tell. Robert laughed, pulled a long strand of spaghetti out of the pot, and said, taste it, is it cooked enough? Should I give it a little longer? —It's good. Tell us! —No. Even though his friends gave him invaluable advice before he set out on his little adventure, he's content to live it all by himself, I said to Lionel. At that same moment, we heard howling music coming from somewhere in the apartment. —What's that? It's Simon, Robert said, he's going to get us kicked out of the building, the little asshole. He abandoned the pasta and went running down the hall. The music stopped cold. We could hear them parleying at great length. He came back with his younger son, who looks like a really nice little boy.

I would have liked to have a son. Robert said, if the neighbors knock on the door, your brother can deal with their shit on his own. And I'll be behind them one hundred percent. What would you like? Some milk? Antoine muttered, some black currant juice. —Not at night, not after brushing your teeth. Black currant juice, Antoine repeated. —Why don't you want milk, you like milk! I want black currant juice, Antoine said. Shit, give the kid some black currant juice, I said, what the hell difference does it make? Robert poured him a glass of black currant juice. —Now go on, buddy, back to bed. Robert drained the spaghetti and poured it into a dish on the table. Lionel said, we had the same problem with Jacob for years. The neighbors spent their lives knocking on our door or ringing our bell. And how is Jacob? Robert asked. Is he still doing that internship in London? Lionel nodded. An internship in what again? I asked. —He's with a record company. —Which one? —It's a small label. —Is he happy? —He seems to be. Robert was busy serving us. He grated some Parmesan cheese. He chopped up some basil and strewed it on the sauce. He set out the condiments, Sicilian olive oil, chili oil. He refilled our glasses. It was good to be together, just us three. I said, it's good to be here, just us three. We drank toasts. To friendship. To old age. To the quality of the old folks' home we were going to wind up in. And let's drink to the rare honor of basking in Lionel's presence, Robert said. Lionel tried to protest. Go on, admit it, I said, he's right, you're never free. It's easier to get an appointment with Nelson Mandela than with Lionel Hutner. Hey, hey, where's your sense of humor, I was just kidding. You're the only one of us who's managed to be happy as part of a couple. I'm sure that takes up a lot of your time. The door opened and there was Simon, Odile and Robert's older boy. A child's body topped by wavy brown locks, mysteriously sticky and brushed down over his forehead, a sign that he was concerned with style. What's the problem now? Robert asked. We'd like not to be disturbed anymore, if that's possible. —Is there any black currant juice left? Oh, wow, pasta, awesome, can I taste it? —Fix yourself a plate and disappear. I contemplated the joy and excitement in the boy's eyes while he stood there in red pajamas he'd grown out of and formed the spaghetti, tomato sauce, and Parmesan into a little mound on his plate. I waited until he picked up his black currant juice with his free hand and left the room, and then I said, he's happy, that's a disposition. You can't be happy in love unless you have a happy disposition. My dear young friend, Robert said, keep it up and you'll manage to ruin the evening. Concentrate on the pasta. Do I hear any compliments? Excellent, Lionel said. —When we die, Anne-Laure and me, the balance sheet will be cataclysmic. But who's going to worry about figures? I will have ruined my life, and I totally won't give a shit. I'm thinking about starting judo in September. I want some pasta too, said Antoine, who had just reappeared. You already ate, you're such a pain in the ass, the two of you, go back to bed, Robert bawled. —Why does Simon get to eat twice? —Because he's twelve. That's bound to convince him, I interjected. Robert grabbed a plate and threw a handful of spaghetti on it. No sauce, just Parmesan, Antoine said. —Go on, get out of here. Robert uncorked another bottle of Brunello. We're not hearing much from you, I said to Lionel. Lionel looked funny. He was staring at the bottom of his glass and turning it in his hand. Then he announced in a sepulchral voice,

Jacob's been committed. Silence followed. He said, he's not in London, he's in a mental clinic in Rueil-Malmaison. Can I count on your complete discretion? Not a word to Anne-Laure, Odile, or anyone else. Of course, Robert and I said. Of course. Robert filled Lionel's glass. Lionel took several consecutive sips. —Do you remember how much he liked...how he was infatuated with...with Céline Dion? As soon as he spoke the name, Lionel broke into a spluttering laugh, an irrepressible laugh, his eyes red and misty, his body shaken by spasms. We were petrified to see him laughing like that. He tried to say something else, but it seemed that all he could do was to repeat that name, never with entire success, because his voice was strangled and every attempt was drowned in a tragic hilarity. He wiped the tears off his cheeks with the palms of his hands. We weren't sure where those tears had come from, whether from laughing or weeping. After a brief while, he calmed down. Robert patted his shoulder. We stayed like that, the three of us, seated around the table. Not understanding anything and not knowing what to do. Eventually Lionel stood up. He ran water in the sink and splashed his face several times. Then he turned to us and said, making a visible effort to utter the words, Jacob imagines he's Céline Dion. He's *convinced* he's Céline Dion. I didn't dare look at Robert. Lionel had spoken that last sentence with extreme solemnity, and he was examining us with terrified eyes. I thought, as long as I don't look at Robert, I can project empathy. As long as I ignore Robert, I can keep the sorrowful mask Lionel needs on my face. He was the happiest child on earth, Lionel said. The most inventive. He'd create landscapes in his room, archipelagos, a zoo, a parking garage. He organized all kinds of shows. Not just music shows. He had a shop where you used fake money. He'd shout, shop's open! I don't know why, but that evocation of Jacob's shop plunged Lionel into an uneasy reverie. He started staring at a point on the tiled floor. Then he said, you're right, you have to be disposed to happiness. Can it be that it's bad to have such a disposition in childhood? I've asked myself that question. Can it be the case that being a happy child doesn't augur well for the rest of your life? As I looked at Lionel, standing there in the middle of the kitchen with his belt cinched too high and his shirt tucked in wrong, I reflected that it didn't take much to make a man look vulnerable. Behind me, Robert said, come back here and sit down, old buddy. I made the mistake of turning toward him. For the length of a second, our eyes met. I don't know which of us cracked first. We hunched over the table, suffocating with laughter. I remember grabbing Robert's arm in an effort to make him stop, I still have the sound of his unruly guffaws in my ears. We got to our feet, still laughing, and implored Lionel to forgive us. Robert took Lionel in his arms, I pressed myself against them, and we embraced him like two ashamed children hiding in their mother's skirts. Then Robert broke away from us. At the price of a level of concentration that I imagine was pretty intense, he'd managed to recompose his features and give himself a serious face again. He said, you know we're not making fun of you. Lionel was magnificent, he smiled amiably and said, I know, I know. Once again, we sat at the table. Robert refilled the glasses. We drank more toasts. To friendship. To Jacob's health. We asked Lionel some questions. He said, Pascaline's been impressive. I know how worried she is, but she maintains a cheerful spirit, she stays positive. Don't tell her you know about this. If she brings up the subject with you someday, you had no idea, he said. We promised not to tell anyone. We tried to talk about something else. Lionel got me started on my recent reporting assignments. I told them about the inauguration of the Jewish memorial center in Skopje, Macedonia. The outdoor ceremony with the attendees sitting on plastic chairs. The sound of a fanfare coming from far away, like the sound of a mechanical toy. The three Macedonian soldiers, skinhead types with shaved skulls, long cloaks, and horizontally outstretched arms, carrying a cushion on which there was something that looked like a soda can and in fact turned out to be an urn containing the ashes of people who died in Treblinka concentration camp. The whole thing completely grotesque. And one month later, fanfare redux in Rwanda. The eighteenth anniversary of the genocide, commemorated in the stadium in Kigali. Guys surging through a gate something like the lions' entrance in *Ben Hur*, goose-stepping and throwing batons. I said, why do all these massacres have to end with fanfares? Yes, good question, Lionel remarked. And we started laughing again, all three of us, probably pretty loaded by then.

Hélène Barnèche

In the bus the other day, a man—quite a corpulent fellow—
sat next to the window on the seat across from mine. It was
a while before I took any interest in him. I raised my head
only because I could feel his eyes on me. He was scrutiniz-
ing me in an immensely serious, almost divinatory way. I did
what one does in such situations, I boldly held his gaze to
demonstrate my indifference and returned to other contem-
plations. But I was uneasy. I felt the persistence of his interest, and I even wondered if I might not toss a remark his
way. I was giving this notion further consideration when I
heard, Hélène? Hélène Barnèche? I said, do we know each
other? He said, as if he was the only one in the world, which
was moreover the case, Igor. It wasn't so much the name
itself as the way he pronounced it that I recognized at once.
A way of drawing out the *o*, of slipping a little pretentious
irony into those two syllables. I repeated the name, stupidly,
and scrutinized his face in my turn. I'm a woman who
doesn't like photographs (I never take any), who doesn't like
any image, whether cheerful or sad, that's capable of rousing
the emotions. Emotions are frightening. I wish that life, as it
advances, would gradually erase everything behind it. I
couldn't connect the new Igor to the one in the past, neither
his physical consistency nor any of the attributes of his
magic. But I remembered the period of time that had borne
his name. When I met Igor Lorrain, I was twenty-six and he

was hardly older. I was already married to Raoul, and I was working as a secretary at the Caisse des Dépôts. Igor was a medical student. At the time, Raoul spent his nights playing cards in the cafés. A friend of his named Yorgos would bring Igor along to the Darcey, a café in Place Clichy. I was there almost every night, but I'd leave early and go home to bed. Igor would offer to give me a ride. He had a little blue Citroën 2CV that had to be started with a crank by opening the hood because the radiator was dented. He was tall and thin. He was hesitating between bridge and psychiatry. And above all, he was crazy. It was hard to resist him. One evening when we were stopped at a red light, he leaned toward me and said, poor Hélène, you're so neglected. And he kissed me. It wasn't true, I didn't feel neglected, but in the time it took me to ask myself whether I was or not I was already in his arms. Neither of us had eaten, so he took me to a bistro near Porte de Saint-Cloud. It didn't take long for me to understand what I was dealing with. He ordered two plates of chicken and green beans. When we were served, he tasted his and said, hold on, put some salt on it. I said, no, I think it's good the way it is. He said, no it's not, it's not salted enough, add some salt. I said, it's fine like this, Igor. He said, I'm telling you, put some salt on it. I put some salt on it. Igor Lorrain came from the North, like me. He was from Béthune. His father worked in river transport. At my house, we never laughed, but his was even worse. In our families, the slaps came hard and fast, when they weren't punches or objects thrown at your head. For a long time I used to get in fights for a yes or a no. I hit my girlfriends, I hit my boyfriends. In the beginning I used to hit Raoul, but he just laughed. I didn't know what else to do when he annoyed me. So I'd whack him one. He'd bend over extravagantly, as though stricken by one of the plagues of Egypt, or else grab both my wrists with one hand and laugh. I never hit Damien. After I had him, I never hit anyone anymore. On bus 95, which goes from Place Clichy to Porte de Vanves, I remembered what had bound me to Igor Lorrain. Not love, not any of the other names for feelings, but savagery. He leaned toward me and said, do you recognize me? Yes and no, I said. He smiled. I remembered that I'd never been able to answer him clearly in the old days either. —Is your name still Hélène Barnèche? —Yes. —Are you still married to Raoul Barnèche? —Yes. I would have liked to answer at greater length, but I couldn't say *tu* to him. He had a fat neck and long, salt-and-pepper hair tied back in a strange way. In his eyes I could still see the potential for dark madness that had captivated me in the past. I gave myself a mental once-over. My hair, my dress and cardigan sweater, my hands. He leaned forward again and said, are you happy? I said yes and I thought, what a nerve. He nodded, putting on a little affectation of tenderness, and said, you're happy, good for you. I felt like smacking him. Thirty years of tranquillity swept aside in ten seconds. I said, and you, Igor? He settled against the back of his seat and answered, me, no. —Are you a psychiatrist? —Psychiatrist and psychoanalyst. I made a face to indicate that I wasn't acquainted with those subtleties. He made a gesture to indicate that they weren't important. He said, where are you going? Those four words knocked me sideways. *Where are you going*, as if we'd seen each other yesterday. And spoken in the same tone as in the old days, as if we'd done nothing in life but go round in circles. *Where are you going* pierced me through and through.

A confusion of feelings clouded my thoughts. There's an abandoned region inside me that craves tyranny. Raoul has never actually *had* me. My Rouli has always thought about gambling and enjoying himself. It's never occurred to him to keep an eye on his little woman. Igor Lorrain wanted to tie me to him. He wanted to know in detail where I was going, what I was doing, and with whom I was doing it. He used to say, you belong to me. I'd say, no I don't. He'd say, tell me you belong to me. I'd say, no. He'd squeeze my throat, squeeze it hard until I said, I belong to you. On other occasions, he'd hit me. I'd have to repeat the words because he hadn't been able to hear them. I'd struggle, I'd trade blows with him, but he always overcame me in the end. We'd wind up in bed, comforting each other. Then I'd run away. He lived in a tiny one-room top-floor apartment on Boulevard Exelmans. I'd run away down the stairs. He'd lean over the banister and shout, say you belong to me, and as I raced on down I'd say, no, no, no. He'd catch up with me and jam me against a wall or the elevator cage (sometimes neighbors would pass), and he'd say, where are you going, you little bitch, you know you belong to me. We'd make love again on the stairs. A woman wants to be dominated. A woman wants to be enslaved. You can't explain that to everyone. I tried to restore the man sitting across from me on the bus. An old, worn-out beau. I didn't recognize the rhythm of his body. But his eyes, yes. And his voice. —Where are you going? —Institut Pasteur. —What are you going to do there? —You're asking too much. —Do you have any children? —A son. —How old? —Twenty-two. And how about you? Do you have children? —What's his name? —My son? Damien. And do you have children? Igor

Lorrain nodded. He looked out the window at a billboard for heating systems. Could he have children? Obviously. Anyone can have children. I would have liked to know what kind of woman he had children with. I wanted to ask him if he was married, but I didn't. I felt sorry for him, and for me. Two people, practically oldsters, lurching around Paris, bearing their lives. On the seat beside him he'd put a threadbare leather case, a sort of briefcase. Its handle was faded. He seemed very much alone. His way of holding himself, his clothes. People can tell when no one looks after you. Maybe he has someone, but not someone who looks after him. Me, I pamper my Rouli. One might even say that I bother him. I choose his clothes, I dye his eyebrows, I stop him from drinking and eating the entire bowl of salted nuts. In my way, I'm alone too. Raoul is sweet and affectionate (except when we're bridge partners, then he undergoes a metamorphosis), but I know he gets bored with me (except when we go to the movies). He's happy with his pals, he's invented an existence for himself outside of ordinary reality and exempt from the duties everyone else has. My friend Chantal says that Raoul's like a politician. Politicians are always absent even when they're there. Damien has moved out. I even forced myself to encourage his exit. While cleaning up his room, I came across remnants from every stage of his life. When I opened a box full of painted chestnuts one evening, I sat on his bed and cried. Children go away, it has to happen, it's normal. Igor Lorrain said, I'm getting off here, come with me. I looked at the name of the stop, which was Rennes-Saint-Placide. I said, I'm getting off at Pasteur-Docteur-Roux. He shrugged his shoulders as if that was the least conceivable destination. He stood up. He said, come, Hélène. *Come, Hélène.* And he reached out his hand. I thought, he's nuts. I thought, we're still alive. I put my hand on his. He drew me through the other passengers to the exit door, and we climbed down off the bus. It was a fine day. Men were working on the roadway. We had to slip through a labyrinth of cinder blocks and particleboards to cross Rue de Rennes. People were rushing in both directions, jostling one another. Everything was very loud. Igor held my hand tight. We ended up on Boulevard Raspail. I was infinitely grateful to him for not letting go of me. The sunlight was blinding. I made out, as if for the first time, the rows of trees lining the boulevard, the plant beds with their blue-green wrought iron fences. I had no idea where we were going. Did he know? One day Igor Lorrain had told me, it was a mistake to put me in a human society. God should have put me in a savanna and made me a tiger. I would have ruled over my territory without mercy. We walked toward Place Denfert-Rochereau. He said, you're still so little. He was as tall as before, but thicker. I had to run a bit to keep up with him.

Jeannette Blot

Awful. Awful. Awful. I don't even want to leave the dressing room to show myself to Marguerite. I can't wear any fitted clothes. I have no more waist. My bust has expanded. I can't display my cleavage. In the past, yes. Today, no. Marguerite's not realistic, not at all. Besides, she herself wears only round necklines or, if not, a modest little scarf. My daughter and my sister-in-law have got it into their heads to dress me for I don't know what psychological purposes. At my seventieth birthday celebration the other evening, Odile said to me, you don't dress, Maman, you cover yourself with fabric. —So what? Who looks at me? Surely not Ernest. Your father doesn't even remember that I have a body. The next day she called to tell me she'd been passing in front of Franck et Fils and she'd seen a little brown dress with orange edging. It would look fabulous on you, Maman, she said. It's true that on the mannequin in the window, the dress has a certain elegance. Does it fit? Marguerite asks from the other side of the curtain. —No, no, not at all! —Show me. —No, no, it's not worth the trouble! I try to take the dress off. The zipper's stuck. I'm just about to tear the whole thing. I step out of the dressing room, a stifling burial chamber, and say, help me take this thing off, Marguerite! —Let me see you. You look great! What don't you like? —I don't like anything. It's completely horrible. Can you make this zipper work? —What about the blouse? —I hate frills. —It doesn't have any. —Yes it does.

—Why are you so nervous, Jeannette? —Because the two of you, you and Odile, are forcing me to do things against my nature. This is torture, this shopping. —The zipper's caught in your slip, stop wriggling around like that. I start to cry. It happens all of a sudden. Marguerite's fussing around behind me. I don't want her to notice my tears. It's absurd. For years on end you swallow all your tears, and then you cry for no reason in a fitting room at Franck et Fils. You OK? says Marguerite. Nothing wrong with her ears. She irritates me, she notices everything. In the end, I've come to prefer people who notice nothing. You learn to be alone. You organize your life quite well. You don't need to explain yourself. Marguerite says, don't move, I'm almost there. In one of Gilbert Cesbron's books, I believe, a woman asks her confessor, should one yield to chagrin, or struggle against it and contain it? Choking back tears doesn't do any good, the confessor replies. Your chagrin remains lodged somewhere. There we are, Marguerite says triumphantly. I retreat behind the curtain to liberate myself. I put my own clothes back on, I try to freshen my face. The dress slides off the hanger and falls, I pick it up and leave it on the stool like a rag. Outside in the street, I urge Marguerite to drop this project of making me care about how I look anymore. My sister-in-law stops in front of every store window. Ready-to-wear shops, shoe shops, leather goods shops, even household linen shops. I must admit she lives in Rouen, poor thing. From time to time, she tries to remotivate me, but it's clear she's the one who wants to go in, touch a purse, try something on. I tell her, that would have looked really good on you, let's go back in and see. She replies, oh no, no, I have too many things I never wear, I don't know what to do with them anymore. I insist, I say, that's a nice little jacket, it would go with anything. Marguerite shakes her head. I'm afraid she's just being tactful. I find this depressing, two women walking past rows of fashionable little shops without wanting anything. I don't dare ask Marguerite if she has a man in her life (that's a stupid expression, what's it supposed to mean, to have a man in your life? I've got one on paper and I still don't have one). When you have a man in your life, you wonder about idiotic things, the condition of your lipstick, the shape of your bra, the color of your hair. That fills up the time. It's fun. Maybe Marguerite has preoccupations of that sort. I could ask her, but I'm afraid of a revelation that will cause me pain. It's been so many years since I aspired to any kind of transformation. When Ernest was at the height of his career, he'd inspect my appearance. It wasn't that he was being attentive. We went out a lot. I was a decorative element. The other day I took my grandson Simon to the Louvre to see the Italian Renaissance paintings. That little boy is the light of my life. At the age of twelve, he's interested in art. As I looked at the pictures, with their figures in dark clothing, the cruel malefactors of olden days, hugging the walls, walking stooped over, headed for who knows where, I said to myself, what becomes of those wicked souls? Have they disappeared from all the books, disappeared with full impunity? I thought about Ernest. Ernest Blot, my husband, is like those twilight shadows. Underhanded, deceitful, pitiless. I must be a little twisted myself for having wanted the love of such a man. Women are seduced by frightful men, because frightful men present themselves in masks, as at a costume ball. They arrive with mandolins and party outfits. I was pretty. Ernest was possessive, and I mistook jealousy for love. I let forty-eight years pass. We live in the illusion of repetition, like the rising and setting sun. We go to bed, we get up, we think we're repeating the same action, but that's not true. Marguerite doesn't resemble her brother. She's amiable, she has scruples. She says, Jeannette, do you still want to try driving? I say, you think I should? You don't think it would be a crazy thing to do? We both start laughing. All of a sudden we're excited. It's been thirty years since I've touched a steering wheel. Marguerite says, we're going to find a place in the Bois de Boulogne, a place where there isn't any traffic. —All right. All right. We look for her car. Marguerite has forgotten where she parked it, and as for me, I've even forgotten what it looks like. I propose two or three to her before we happen upon the right one. She turns on the ignition and we're off. I observe her movements. She asks, have you brought your driver's license? —Yes. You think it's still valid? This kind of license doesn't exist anymore. Marguerite gives it a quick look and says, I have the same kind. —What kind of car is this? —A Peugeot 207. Automatic shift. —An automatic! I can't drive an automatic! —It's very easy. There's nothing to do. —Oh, dear, an automatic! Marguerite says, you won't tell Odile anything, you promise, right? I don't want to get chewed out by your daughter. —I won't tell her anything. She gets on my nerves, Odile, being so overprotective. I'm not made of glass. We drive around the Bois for a while, looking for an out-of-the-way spot with no traffic. Eventually we find a little lane blocked after some distance by a white gate about fifteen feet wide. Marguerite parks. She turns off the switch. We both get out so we can change sides. We laugh a little. I say, I don't know anything about driving anymore, Marguerite. She says, you have two pedals. The brake and the accelerator. You use only your right foot to press on them. Your left foot has nothing to do. Start the car. I start the car. The engine purrs. I turn to Marguerite, enthused by having started the car so easily. Very good, says Marguerite in her professorial voice (she teaches Spanish). You were able to start the engine because the shift's in P, which stands for Park. Put your seat belt on. —You think? —Yes, yes. Marguerite leans over and fastens the seat belt, which seems really tight. I say, I feel like a prisoner. —You'll get used to it. Now move the gear shift to D as in Drive. Where's your right foot? —Nowhere. —Put it on the brake. —Why? —Because once the car's in Drive, when you take your foot off the brake we'll start to move. —You think? —Yes. —My foot's there. —Move the lever to D. I take a deep breath and move the lever to D. Nothing happens. Marguerite says, now slowly take your foot off the pedal. Go on, go on, release the pedal completely. I release the pedal completely. I'm extremely tense. The car starts moving. I say, it's moving! —Now put your foot on the accelerator. —Where is it? —Right next to the brake, right next to it. I poke around with my foot, I feel a pedal, I press it. The car stops violently, throwing us forward. The seat belt slices into my chest. What's happening? —You hit the brake again and killed the engine. We'll start over. Shift into P, Park. Start the car. Bravo. Now, move the shift to N. —What's N? —Neutral. No gear. Nothing. —Ah, nothing. Right, right. —Let's try again. Right foot on the brake. Gear shift to D. Relax your left foot, it doesn't have anything to do. —I can't drive an automatic! —Yes you can. Look. Put the shift on D and take your foot off the brake. Bravo. Now move your foot slightly to the right, find the accelerator pedal, and press on it. I concentrate. The car's rolling. I hold my breath. The gate's still pretty far away, but I'm heading for it without any control over anything. I panic. How do I brake? How do I stop? —Put your foot on the brake. —I stay in…in…what's it called? —Yes, you stay in Drive. And the moment the car stops, you shift back to N. N, not R! R means Reverse, for backing up. Don't use your left foot! You're pressing on both pedals at the same time, Jeannette! We come to a jolting halt, accompanied by a strange noise. I'm soaked. I say, I hope you have more patience with your students. —My students are quicker. —You're the one who thought I should take up driving again. —You mope around in your apartment all day long, you need some independence. Start the engine again. Shift into P first. What's your right foot doing? —I don't know. —Put it on the accelerator, but don't press down. There. Move the shift to D. And go. Accelerate slowly. My sister-in-law's instructions hurry off to some remote part of my brain. I respond to them mechanically. The little ball of chagrin has returned to my throat. I try to get rid of it. We're moving forward. Where are you going? Marguerite asks. —I don't know. —You're headed straight for the gate. —Yes. —You can turn off onto the grass. Make a circle around that tree there and go back the way we came. She points out a place I don't see because I'm incapable of looking anywhere but straight ahead. Slow down, Marguerite says, slow down. She stresses me. I can't remember how to slow down anymore. My arms are bolted to the steering wheel like two steel bars. Turn off, turn off, Jeannette! Marguerite cries. I don't know where I am anymore. Marguerite has grabbed the steering wheel. The gate's six feet away. —Let go of the wheel, Jeannette! Take your foot off the gas! She pulls the hand brake and moves the shift lever. The car rears, hits the white gate, scrapes along it, and then stops moving altogether. Marguerite doesn't say a word. My tears have welled up all at once, and they're blurring my vision. Marguerite gets out. She walks around the back of the car to check the damage. Then she opens my door. In a gentle voice (which is worse than everything else), she says, come, get out, I'm going to back the car up a bit. She helps me take off the seat belt. She sits in my seat and backs up a short way to separate the 207 from the gate. She gets out again. The left front is a little dented, the headlight's broken, and the whole left fender is scratched. I murmur, I'm really sorry, forgive me. Marguerite says, you did a good job on it, no question about that. —I'm really sorry, Marguerite, I'll pay for the repairs. She looks at me and says, Jeannette, you're not going to cry over this, are you? Jeannette, dear, that's ridiculous, who cares about a dented car? If you knew the number of things I've crashed into in my time. Not only that, I nearly ran over a seventh grader in front of the lycée one day. I say, forgive me, forgive me, I've spoiled the whole day. Come on, get back in, says Marguerite, let's go get some ice cream at Bagatelle. I've been wanting to go back to Bagatelle for months. We take our original places in the car. She starts it at once and backs up onto the grass with a dexterity that grieves me. I understand people who like bad weather. Bad weather doesn't give you ideas about going to visit a flower garden. Buck up, Jeannette, Marguerite says. There's no denying that gate was holding out its arms to us. To tell you the truth, I knew from the start you were going to run into it. I smile in spite of myself. I say, you'll never tell Ernest about this, right? Aha, I've got you now, Marguerite says, laughing. I adore Marguerite. I'd rather have married her than her brother. I hear my cell phone ringing in my purse. Odile installed an unusually piercing ring tone for me because she thinks I'm deaf. Apart from Odile, Ernest, and my son-in-law Robert, nobody calls me on that phone. —Hello? —Maman? —Yes? —Where are you? —In the Bois de Boulogne. —Good. Now don't worry, but Papa was having lunch with his pals from the Third Circle and he blacked out. The restaurant called an ambulance. They took him to the Pitié. —He blacked out? —Are you still with Marguerite? —Yes... —Did you two find some nice things? I say, what do you mean, blacked out? And where are you, Odile? Odile's voice is muffled and a bit sepulchral. —I'm at the Pitié-Salpêtrière Hospital. They're going to perform a coronary angiogram to see if his bypasses are blocked. —To see what? They're going to do what to him? —We'll just wait for the results. Don't worry. And tell me, did you try on that dress at Franck et Fils, Maman?

Robert Toscano

All of a sudden, as we're leaving the hospital morgue (known as the Amphitheater) on Rue Bruant, at the moment when the men are shoving Ernest's coffin into the back of the funeral coach, my mother-in-law Jeannette, seized by some incomprehensible terror, refuses to get into the vehicle. She's supposed to sit in the front with Marguerite and the funeral director—today called the master of ceremonies— and Odile, my mother, and I are supposed to follow them in the Volkswagen to the crematorium in Père-Lachaise Cemetery. Wearing high-heeled shoes never before seen on her feet, my mother-in-law retreats (nearly falling down as she does) to the wall, like an animal about to be led to the slaughterhouse. With her back pressed against the stone in the dazzling sunlight, she enjoins the driver of the coach, a big Mercedes station wagon, to go on without her, all the while making frenetic, sweeping gestures before the alarmed eyes of Ernest's sister Marguerite, who's already installed in the backseat. Maman, Maman, Odile says, if you don't want to ride with Papa, I'll go instead. She gently takes Jeannette's arm to guide her to the Volkswagen, where my mother, wilting in the heat (summer has arrived all at once), is sitting in the front seat, waiting. The director hastens to open the rear door, but Jeannette babbles something that turns out to be, I want to sit in front. Odile whispers, Maman, please, that's not important. —I want to follow Ernest. That's my husband in there! If you want me to stay with you, Maman, Marguerite can ride with the coffin by herself, Odile says, giving me a look that means, get your mother to change places. No doubt I fail to react properly, because Odile thrusts her head into the car and says, Zozo, would you be kind enough to sit in the backseat? The idea of getting into the funeral coach is making Maman anxious. My mother looks at me with the expression of a person who believes that she has now seen everything. Without a word, slowly, she unfastens her seat belt, collects her purse, and extracts herself from the front seat, emphasizing the arthritic discomfort of the movements. Thanks, Zozo, Odile says, that's very generous of you. Still unspeaking, and with the same heaviness in her body language, my mother ensconces herself in the backseat. Jeannette sits in the front without any acknowledgment, and in any case she looks like someone who has no more place in this world. Odile gets into the Mercedes with her aunt and the funeral director. I take the wheel of the Volkswagen and proceed to follow them to Père-Lachaise. After a moment, Jeannette, her face to the windshield and her eyes riveted on the black hatch of the Mercedes, says, was your husband cremated, Zozo? Cremated? my mother repeats. I say incinerate. No, says Jeannette, you use incinerate for household garbage. The things I learn, my mother says. My father's buried in Bagneux cemetery, I say, intervening. Jeannette seems to ponder this information, and then she turns around and asks my mother, will you have yourself buried with him? Good question, says my mother. If it was up to me, not in this life. I hate that Bagneux. Nobody ever comes to see you. It's completely in the sticks. In front of us, the Mercedes crawls along at an exasperatingly slow pace. Is that part of the ceremony? We stop at a red light. A vague silence has set in. I'm hot. My tie's strangling me. The suit I'm wearing is too heavy. Jeannette's looking for something in her purse. I can't stand the semimuffled noises, the clinking and the leather-creaking that accompany her rummaging around. All the more so as she's sighing, and I can't stand people who sigh either. After a moment, I ask, what are you looking for, Jeannette? —The obituary in *Le Monde*, I didn't even have time to look at it. I thrust my right hand into her purse and help her extract the folded, crumpled article. —Can you read it out loud? Jeannette puts on her glasses and reads in a dismal voice: "Ernest Blot Dies. A banker both influential and secretive. Born in 1939, Ernest Blot died in the night of June 23 at the age of seventy-three. His demise marks the passing of a leading figure in French elite banking, one of those whose career began in the civil service and whose savoir-faire was equaled only by his discretion. In 1965, he graduated with top honors from the National School of Administration"—top honors, you see, I'd forgotten about that—"and joined the General Inspection of Finances. Between 1969 and 1978, he was a member of several ministerial cabinets, serving as technical consultant," et cetera, we know all that... "In 1979, he joined the Wurmster Bank, which had been founded just after the First World War and had since fallen somewhat into obsolescence. He was the bank's director general until 1985, when he became its chairman and chief executive officer. Little by little, he turned the Wurmster Bank into one of France's premier institutions, on a par with Lazard Frères or the Rothschild banking houses..."—et cetera—"He was the author of a biography of Achille Fould, Minister of Finance in the Second Republic

(Éditions Perrin, 1997). Ernest Blot held the rank of Grand Officer in the National Order of Merit and was a Commander in the Legion of Honor..." Not a word about his wife, Jeannette observes. Is that the usual procedure? As for the Achille Fould, I never once opened it. It sold three copies. I feel nauseous after reading all that. My mother says, it's stifling in this car, will you turn up the AC, darling? No AC! Jeannette screams, no AC, it makes my head throb. I look at the rearview mirror. So as not to contradict the widow of the day, my mother has rearranged herself by simply throwing back her head and opening her mouth like a carp out of water. Jeannette reaches into her purse again and pulls out a battery-operated pocket fan with transparent blades. —Here, Zozo, this will cool you off. She turns it on. It makes a sound like a maddened wasp. Jeannette describes two circles around her own face and holds out the fan to my mother. —Try it, Zozo, it really works. —No, thanks. —Take it, Maman, you're hot. —I'm fine, stop bugging me. Jeannette makes another little pass with the fan from one side of her neck to the other. In a cavernous voice right behind my ear, my mother says, I still blame your father for not selling that pathetic burial plot. When I die, Robert, have us moved. Put us in the city. Paulette told me there are still some places in the Jewish section in Montparnasse cemetery. The Mercedes turns left, describing a kind of majestic circle and fleetingly revealing the mute profiles of Odile and Marguerite. Jeannette says, I don't feel anything at all. She seems lost. Her arms are at her sides, her open purse on her lap, the buzzing fan in one inert hand. I feel I should reply to her, make some comment, but nothing comes to me. Ernest occupied an important place in my life. He was interested in my work (I'd read certain articles to him before submitting them to the newspaper). He'd question me and dispute with me the way I would have liked my own father to do (my father was kind and affectionate, but he didn't know how to be a grown man's father). We'd call each other almost every morning to fix Syria and Iran and criticize Western naïveté and European conceit. That was his hobbyhorse: the fact that now, after a thousand years of massacres, we have license to lecture everybody else. I've lost a friend who had a vision of existence. That's pretty rare. People don't have a vision of existence. They have nothing but opinions. To speak with Ernest was to be less alone. I know their day-to-day marriage couldn't have been much fun for Jeannette. One day—Ernest was leaving for a monetary conference—she threw a cup of coffee at his head. You're a vile character, she said, you've wrecked my life as a woman. Ernest, who was wiping coffee off his suit jacket, replied, your life as a woman? What's that, a life as a woman? After I met Odile, he told me, I give you fair warning, she's a pain in the ass, I'll thank you if you take her off my hands. And later he said, don't worry, my boy, the first marriage is always hard. I asked him, have you been married more than once? —No, that's just it. I hear my mother talking in the backseat. It takes me a couple of moments to come back from my thoughts and understand her words. She's saying, it's afterward that you feel something, when all the pomp and fuss of death is over. When the pomp and fuss is over, Jeannette says, I'll feel nothing but resentment. You're exaggerating, I say. She shakes her head and asks, was he a good husband, yours, Zozo? Ooohh… says my mother. —What are you trying to say, Maman? You were happy with Papa, weren't you? —I wasn't unhappy. That wasn't it. But you know, good husbands are few and far between. We drive along Avenue Gambetta in silence. The trees cast swaying shadows. Jeannette has started digging in her purse again. A driver on my left blows his horn. The car pulls even with us and I'm on the verge of replying with some insult when I recognize the Hutners' smiling (in the proper funeral manner) faces. Lionel's driving. Pascaline's leaning out of the window and making hand signals to Jeannette. I glance briefly at the rear of their car. Before I accelerate, I have time to notice their son Jacob sitting in the backseat, grave and ramrod-straight, with some kind of Indian scarf wrapped around his neck. You invited the Hutners? Jeannette asks in a crushed voice. —We invited our closest friends. The Hutners were very fond of Ernest. —Oh my God, it kills me to talk to all these people, all this kills me. This society gathering. For this crappy cremation. She pulls down the sun visor with the mirror and checks her face. As she's putting on lipstick, she says, you know who *I* invited? Raoul Barnèche. —Who's that? —There's something none of you knows, not even Odile, something that won't appear in any newspaper. I had to put up with it on my own. When Ernest came home from his bypass surgery in 2002, he fell into a black hole and stayed there. He was down, morning and night, prostrated in the big chair under the unicorn painting, picking at his food, refusing to do any therapy. He thought he was through. Albert, his chauffeur, had the idea of introducing his brother to Ernest. His brother's Raoul Barnèche, a champion card player. And a handsome man, as you'll see, a Robert Mitchum type. He started coming over almost every day to play gin rummy with Ernest. They played for money. The stakes got higher and higher. That brought Ernest back to life. I had to call a halt before he got completely taken to the cleaners. But the cards saved him. We turn into the cemetery from Rue des Rondeaux, on the side where the funerary chapel is. The Mercedes comes to a stop in front of the Neo-Byzantine crematorium. There are people on the steps and among the columns. I share Jeannette's anxiety. Odile and Marguerite are already standing outside the car. A man dressed in black points me to the parking area on the left. I say to the women, do you want to get out here first? They both say no and I understand why. I park the car. We walk along the side of the building. Odile comes to meet her mother. She says, there are more than a hundred people here, and the chapel doors are still closed. I notice Paola Suares, the Condamines, the Hutners, Marguerite's children, and Doctor Ayoun, to whose office I accompanied Ernest on several occasions. I see Jean Ehrenfried climb up the steps one by one, supported by Darius Ardashir, who's also carrying Jean's crutch. A little apart, near a bush, I recognize Albert, my late father-in-law's chauffeur. Jeannette smiles at the man he's with, a fellow wearing mafioso sunglasses. The two of them come over to us. Albert puts his arms around my mother-in-law. When he releases her, his eyes are damp and his face seems to have shrunk. He says, twenty-seven years. Jeannette repeats the number. I ask myself if Jeannette is aware of how much Albert could have seen and hidden from her in the course of those twenty-seven years. She turns toward the other man. He's dark-haired, wearing a corduroy jacket. Jeannette takes his hand and says, it was so kind of you to come, Raoul. The man takes off his sunglasses and says, I was moved, sincerely moved. Jeannette doesn't release his hand. She gives it a series of little shakes. He lets her, though he's somewhat embarrassed. She says, Raoul Barnèche. He and Ernest used to play gin rummy together. It's true, I think, there's something Robert Mitchum–like about him. His dimpled chin, his sleepy eyes, his wayward hair. Jeannette's rosy all over. He smiles. In the area in front of the crematorium, under a uniformly blue sky, while family, friends, and officials wait for her, my mother-in-law stubbornly clings to this man whose name I've never heard before. I sense movement around us. Through the columns, I see the doors of the chapel open. I look for my mother, who has vanished. I spot her standing with the Hutners at the foot of the steps and go over to her. Odile joins us. She kisses Jacob warmly and says, I haven't seen you for so long, have you grown since the last time? In a thin voice and with a pronounced Québécois accent, Jacob says, Odile, you know I lost my father too, of course it's been very difficult, but I've made a place for him at the bottom of my heart. He places his hands on his chest and adds, I know he's here with me. Odile gives me a bewildered look. I bat my eyelids soothingly and form the words *I'll explain later* with my lips. I step next to Lionel, whose face has turned to stone, take his arm, and set my mother in motion with my other hand. She's about to make a comment as we go up the steps, but I compel her to refrain by squeezing her arm. The chapel is filling up in silence. I seat my mother and the Hutners and go off to play my role as host among the rows of seats. I greet members of the family, a number of Ernest's Breton cousins, André Taneux, Ernest's fellow student at the ENA and the first president of the Court of Auditors, the publisher of my newspaper (whose ridiculous three-day beard Odile approves of), several strangers, the finance minister's chief of staff, the head of the

General Inspection of Finances, and some of Ernest's former colleagues in the Inspection, who slip spontaneously into the rows. Darius Ardashir introduces me to the president of the Third Circle's board of governors. I come across Odile again, this time among the staff of the Wurmster Bank. She's wearing her little power hairdo, her Counselor Toscano look. She's putting up a brave front. She murmurs into my ear, Jacob?! I don't have time to reply, because the master of ceremonies asks us to take our seats in the first row, where Marguerite, her children, and Jeannette are already sitting. The company rises. Ernest's coffin has entered the nave of the chapel. The bearers place the coffin on the trestles at the foot of the steps leading up to the catafalque. The funeral director steps to the lectern. At the top of the double flight of stairs behind him, in the painting that surrounds the platform, a city half Jerusalem and half Babel, with biblical poplars scattered here and there, is bathed in a starry, blue, supremely kitschy twilight. The funeral director proposes a few moments of silence. I imagine Ernest, lying there in his tight Lanvin suit, a leftover from the 1960s that Jeannette chose for the occasion. I'll be there too one day, I think, I too will stifle in the strongbox of death, completely alone. And so will Odile. And the children. And everybody here, high and low, more or less old, more or less happy, doggedly holding their own in the ranks of the living. And all of them completely alone. Ernest wore that suit for years. Even when it had completely gone out of fashion, even when his belly should have put anything double-breasted out of the question. While driving himself home from Brussels one day, zooming along at 110 miles per hour, Ernest ate a bag of barbecue-flavored potato chips, a chicken sandwich, and a nougat bar. Less than five minutes later, he turned into a cane toad, suffocated by his Lanvin suit and his seat belt. His car was a Peugeot convertible, and as he was entering Paris, a pigeon shit on him. I look for the Hutners. They've moved to the end of their row, just in front of the Condamines. Jacob's on the very end. Looking humble and reserved, I notice, like a person who doesn't wish to attract attention. André Taneux has replaced the master of ceremonies at the lectern. Blow-dried, brushed-back, high-standing hair dyed a radical shade of brown (slightly purple in the diffused light from the stained-glass windows). Odile and Jeannette had been reluctant to let him speak, but he'd seemed quite determined to express himself. He slowly unfolds a sheet of paper, uselessly readjusts the microphone, begins to read: "An imposing silhouette abruptly moves away, leaving in its wake a scent of Gauloises and aristocracy. Ernest Blot has left us. If I come here today to make my voice heard—thank you so much for your permission, Jeannette—it's because with the passing of Ernest Blot, we haven't simply lost a loved one. We've lost a happy moment in our history. In the immediate postwar years, with much of France in ruins, there unexpectedly arose a party capable of reuniting people of all backgrounds and all convictions, believers and atheists, left and right: the party of modernization. Its necessary task was, at one and the same time, to reconstruct both the State and the fabric of enterprise, to build up savings again and place them in the service of growth. Our friend Ernest Blot was one of the emblematic figures in that party. ENA, Inspection of Finances, ministerial cabinets, elite bank: a life lived in a straight, unbroken line, in a period that alas no longer exists, a time when alumni of the National School of

Administration were not technocrats but builders, when the State was marked not by conservatism but by progress, when banks meant not the gambling of wild sums of money in a globalized casino but the stubborn financing of the productive base. It was a period when men of talent dedicated themselves not to making their career or their fortune but to serving their country, in public and private, without venality and without vanity. I feel deep sorrow at having lost Ernest, but I console myself with the thought that a great gentleman has left a world that no longer resembles him. Rest in peace, my friend, remote from a time unworthy of you." And you'd better hurry back to the hair colorist, I say just for Odile to hear. Taneux refolds his sheet of paper, clamps his lips together in grief, and returns to his seat. The funeral director waits for the echo of his footsteps on the marble floor to subside. The director lets another moment pass and then announces, Monsieur Jean Ehrenfried, administrator and business executive, formerly chairman of the board of Safranz-Ulm Electric. Darius Ardashir is leaning over Jean to help him rise to his feet and support himself on his crutch. With cautious, limping steps, Jean moves toward the lectern. He's thin and pale, wearing a checked beige suit and a tie with yellow polka dots. He puts his free hand on the top of the lectern to assure his balance. The wood creaks and resounds. Jean looks at the coffin and then turns his eyes to the assembly. He takes out no sheet of paper, puts on no eyeglasses. "Ernest...you used to ask me, what in the world can I say about you at your funeral? And I'd reply, you're going to sing the praises of an old, stateless Jew, try to say something with some depth for once in your life. I was older than you, and sicker, we didn't anticipate that the situation would be reversed...We spoke regularly on the telephone. The phrase that kept being repeated was, where are you? Where are you? Our work took us to many disparate places, but you had Plou-Gouzan L'Ic, your house near Saint-Brieuc. You had your house and your apple trees, in a little valley. When I said, where are you, and you answered, at Plou-Gouzan L'Ic, I would envy you. You really *were* somewhere. You had forty apple trees. You produced one hundred and twenty liters of cider per year, frightful stuff I eventually came around to thinking was good..." He stops talking. He sways and holds on to the lectern. The funeral director seems to want to intervene, but Jean prevents him and goes on. "It was, to use your own words, a hard, rough cider, put up in plastic bottles with detergent bottle caps, a far cry from the corked, fizzy ciders of the bourgeoisie. It was your cider. It came from your apples, from your land...Where are you now? Where are you? I know your body's in this casket, six feet away. But you, where are you? Not long ago, in my doctor's waiting room, one of his other patients said this: After a while, even life is an idiotic value. It's true that at the end of the road, you fluctuate between the temptation to oppose death energetically—I recently bought a stationary bicycle—and the desire to let yourself slide down into the dark, unknown place... Are you waiting for me somewhere, Ernest...? Where...?" This last word might not be what he says. It's barely audible and could just as well be the first syllable of an unfinished phrase. Jean falls silent. In several tiny stages, careful to dissemble his physical weakness, he turns almost entirely toward the coffin. His lips open and close like a famished bird's beak. His right hand firmly clasps his crutch, and he sways on its pivot. He remains in this precarious position for a long time, murmuring, as it were, into the dead man's ear. Then he looks over in Darius's direction. Darius immediately comes to help him return to his seat. I squeeze Odile's hand, and I see that she's crying. The director, back at the microphone, announces that Ernest Blot's coffin will now be transferred for cremation, which, he adds, is in accordance with the wishes expressed by Monsieur Blot himself. The bearers raise the coffin again. They climb the stairs in silence and reach the catafalque, which looks ridiculously high and far away. A mechanism goes into operation. Ernest disappears.

Odile Toscano

In the last year of her life, your grandmother was a little out of her mind, Marguerite says. She wanted to go into the village and fetch her children. I'd say, Maman, you don't have little children anymore. Yes I do, yes I do, she'd say, I have to get them and bring them home. We'd go looking for her children in Petit-Quevilly. It was a way for me to get her to walk. And it was funny, going to look for Ernest and me as we'd been sixty years before. We've just passed Rennes. Marguerite's sitting by the window next to Robert. Since this trip began, hers has been practically the only voice anyone has heard. Since our two companions have withdrawn opaquely into themselves, my aunt addresses no one but me, in sporadic bursts, exhuming various episodes from the past lives of the dead. We're in one of those new, modern train compartments that are open to the aisle. Maman's sitting next to me and across from Marguerite. She's wedged the Go Sport bag between us. She didn't want to put it up on the rack above our heads. Robert's been sulking ever since he found out we have to change trains at Guingamp. It's my secretary's mistake. She got us round-trip tickets, Paris–Guernonzé, but with a change on the way there. By the time Robert noticed, we were already in Gare Montparnasse, and he accused us of always wanting to complicate things when it would have been so much simpler to take the car. He walked ahead of us on the platform, being obnoxious and carrying the black-and-pink-striped Go Sport bag with the cinerary urn inside. I have no clue about the choice of that bag. Neither does Marguerite. She asks me on the sly, why has your mother put Ernest in that thing? They didn't have something more elegant, like an overnight bag? Outside the window, warehouses go by, along with scattered, dreary industrial zones. Farther on we pass housing developments and then fields of turned earth. I can't figure out how to adjust the back of my seat. It feels as though it's projecting me forward. Robert asks me what I'm trying to do. I'm disturbing his reading, a biography of Hannibal. There's an inscription on the cover, a line from Juvenal: "Weigh Hannibal's ashes: how many pounds will the great general come to?" Maman has closed her eyes. With her hands on her thighs, she lets the train's movements rock her to sleep. Her skirt's too high up on her blouse, which she's tucked in all wrong. It's been a long time since I really looked at her. A portly, weary lady to whom no one pays any attention. In Cabourg, when I was little, she'd walk along the promenade in a tight-waisted muslin dress. The pale fabric would float in the sea breeze, and she'd swing her canvas tote bag. The train passes Lamballe without stopping. We have time to see the railroad parking lot, the doctor's red house! (Marguerite says to us almost yelling), the buildings of the train station, the fortified church. All the shapes are blurred by the treacherous fog. I think about Papa, ground up and inside a gym bag, passing though his childhood town for the last time. I feel like seeing Rémi. I feel like having some fun. What if I experimented with nipple clamps like Paola? Poor Paola. Luc drags her around here and there—I wonder if Robert knows that? If I were a generous friend, I'd introduce her to

Rémi Grobe. They'd like each other. But I want to keep Rémi for myself. Rémi saves me from Robert, from time, from all kinds of melancholy. Last night Robert and I stayed awake in the dark for a long while without speaking. At one point I said, so what's Lionel for Jacob now? I felt Robert considering the question, and I could tell he didn't know the answer. The train stops in Saint-Brieuc. A long ribbon of white houses, all the same. A freight car from the cooperative *Starlette de Plouaret-Bretagne* stands alone on a track in the yard, some distance from the platform. The poor Hutners. But at the same time, could something like that happen to anyone else? The train starts again. Marguerite says, next stop, Guingamp. When we used to go to Plou-Gouzan L'Ic, we'd get off the train in Saint-Brieuc. I've never gone past it. Papa never took me beyond Plou-Gouzan L'Ic, the backwater where he bought the moldy old house he loved and Maman and I detested. The person who supplied the handcuffs and nipple clamps was Luc, Paola told me. Such ideas don't occur to Rémi. And there's no way I'm going to buy the things myself. Online? And I'll have the package sent where? Guingamp, Marguerite cries. We leap to our feet as though the train's not going to stay still for more than five and a half seconds. Robert picks up the Go Sport bag. Marguerite and Maman make a rush for the doors. We get off the train. Guingamp station. On the platform, a glass shelter, and on that a sign for Brest. Marguerite says, we stay here. A damp breeze slips down my neck. I say, it's cold. Marguerite protests. She doesn't want anyone criticizing Brittany. She's wearing a mauve suit buttoned up to her chin. A silk scarf covers her shoulders. She's been as careful about her look as if she were going to a romantic rendezvous. In the center of the platform, inside the glass cage, people are lined up on the only bench. Wan travelers, jammed against one another in front of a pile of luggage. I say, Maman, do you want to sit down? —In there? Surely not. She puts on her overcoat. Robert assists her. She's chosen flat shoes for this occasion. She looks toward the old-fashioned clock and then at the sky, at slowly moving clouds going somewhere. She says, you know what I'm thinking about? My little Austrian pine tree. I'd love to see what it's looking like now. Maman once planted an Austrian pine among the apple trees at Plou-Gouzan L'Ic. Papa said, your mother thinks she's eternal. She bought a six-inch-high seedling because it was cheaper; she thinks she'll still be there, walking around with Simon's great-grandchildren. Robert said, Jeannette, with a little luck, right now that tree's as high as your shoulder—provided it hasn't been uprooted with the weeds. We laugh. I think I hear Papa laughing in the gym bag. Maman eventually says, maybe it didn't have enough room to grow among all those apple trees. Robert walks off, heading for the end of the platform. The back of his suit jacket is wrinkled. He walks parallel to the tracks, still carrying the object of our trip, rolling from one foot to the other, looking for some undefined panorama to contemplate from the empty plat-form. The train we board for the Guingamp–Guernonzé run makes old-time railroad sounds. Its windows are dirty. We pass shacks and grain silos, and then our view is blocked by the guardrail and the bushes. None of us says very much. Robert has put Hannibal away (a few days ago, speaking of him, Robert said this: what a marvelous person) and is busy with his BlackBerry. Guernonzé. The sky has cleared. We leave the station and step out onto a parking lot surrounded by white buildings with gray roofs. There's an Ibis hotel on the other side of the station square. Marguerite says, it wasn't like this at all. Various vehicles are parked in the middle of a profusion of traffic cones, streetlamps, and young trees imprisoned inside wooden pickets. None of this was here before, says Marguerite. Including the Ibis. This is all very recent. She takes Maman's arm. We cross the traffic circle and go up a narrow sidewalk, past deserted houses with closed shutters. The street curves. Cars come from both directions and brush us as they pass. There's the bridge, Marguerite says. —The bridge? —The bridge over the Braive. I'm vexed to discover that it's so close to the train station. I imagined our procession would take longer to arrive. Marguerite shows us a building on the other side of the street and says, your grandparents' house was right behind that. Half of it was torn down, and the rest is a dry cleaner's now. Do you want to see it? —Not worth the trouble. —Where that building is was a garden with a washhouse on the Braive. We used to play there. I say, you spent all your holidays in Guernonzé? —Summers. And Easters. But Easters were sad. The bridge is framed by black, iron guardrails. Containers of blooming flowers hang from the rails. Cars cross the bridge in an endless stream. In the distance, a more or less man-made hill makes Marguerite say, there used to be nothing but green up there. Is this where we're going to scatter the ashes? Maman asks. If you want, says Marguerite. Me? I don't want anything at all, Maman says. —This is where we scattered Papa's ashes. —Why not on the other side? It's prettier. Because the current flows in this direction, Robert says. I believe that real estate agency is brand new, Marguerite says, pointing at the street that runs along the opposite bank of the Braive.

Marguerite, please, stop telling us what things were here before and what things weren't, nobody gives a damn about that, it's not interesting, Maman says. Marguerite scowls. I can't think of anything soothing to say because I agree with Maman. Robert opens the Go Sport bag and takes out the metal urn. Maman looks in all directions and says, it's awful to do this in broad daylight, in the middle of all this traffic. —We don't have a choice, Maman. —This is ridiculous. Robert asks, who's doing it? You, Robert, you, Maman says. Why not Odile? Marguerite says. —Robert will do it better. Robert holds out the urn to me. I can't touch it. It's been impossible for me to lay a finger on that object ever since they handed it over to us at the crematorium. I say, she's right, you do it. Robert opens the outer lid and gives it to me. I chuck it into the bag. He unscrews the inner lid but doesn't remove it. He raises his arms over the balustrade. The two women press against each other like frightened birds. Robert takes off the inner lid and turns the urn upside down. A sort of gray sawdust spills out, disperses in the air, and falls into the Braive. Robert holds me close. We look at the calm river, streaked with wavelets, and the trees on its banks, lengthening into black spots. Behind our backs, the traffic keeps passing, getting louder and louder. Marguerite reaches into one of the hanging planters, plucks a flower, and throws it. The flower's too light. It drifts off to the left, and as soon as it lands in the water, it gets wedged against a pile of stones. Beyond a footbridge, some children are getting ready to go canoeing. What do we do with the urn? Maman asks. We throw it away, says Robert, putting it back in the bag. —Where? —In a trash can. There's one against the wall over there. I suggest we go back to the station. I'll buy us drinks while we're waiting for the train. We leave the bridge. I look at the water, the line of yellow buoys. I say good-bye to Papa. I form a little kiss with my lips. When we reach the wall, Robert tries to fit the Go Sport bag into the trash bin on the corner. —What are you doing, Robert? Why are you throwing that bag away? —This bag is hideous. You're not going to do anything with it, Jeannette. —Yes I will. I use it to carry things. Don't throw it away. I intervene and say, Maman, that bag contained Papa's ashes, it can't serve any further purpose. That's complete nonsense, Maman says, the bag was used to carry a vase, period. Robert, please take out that nasty urn, throw it away, and give the bag back to me. —Maman, that bag cost ten euros! —I want my bag back. —Why? —Because! I was stupid enough to come this far, now I'd like to make a few decisions of my own. Your father's in his river, everything's perfect, and as for me, I'm going back to Paris with my bag. Give me the bag, Robert. Robert has emptied the bag, and he holds it out to Maman. I snatch it away from him and say, Maman, please, this is grotesque. Maman takes hold of the handle and wails, it's my bag, Odile! I shout, this piece of shit is staying in Guernonzé! I jam it deep inside the trash can by the wall. We hear an abrupt, heartrending sob. Marguerite, with raised hands, is offering her face to the sky like a pietà. I myself start to cry. There's the result, well done, Maman says. Robert tries to calm her down and lead her away from the trash bin. She struggles a little, and then, hanging on to his arm, she consents to being guided back along the narrow sidewalk, almost staggering, her body grazing the stone wall. I watch them as they walk, him with his overlong hair and his rumpled back, Hannibal sticking out of his pocket, and her with her flat shoes, her skirt longer than her overcoat, and it occurs to me that of the two of them, Robert is the more bereft. Marguerite blows her nose. She's one of those women who still keeps a handkerchief tucked into a sleeve, ready for use. I kiss her. I take her hand. Her warm fingers wrap around my palm and squeeze. We walk up the sidewalk, a few meters behind Maman and Robert. At the end of the street, as we're coming to the train station's parking lot, Marguerite stops in front of a low house whose openings are framed with red bricks. She says, this is the spot where Ernest ended up in *The Battle of the Rails*. —Here? —Yes. Your grandparents told me about it, I wasn't born yet. He put himself over there, among the extras, in front of a bar that doesn't exist anymore. They were filming a hay wagon. Ernest stood right behind it. He figured at least his legs would be visible. We catch up with Robert and Maman at the intersection. He saw that movie five or six times, Marguerite says. Even when he was an old man—you were a witness, Jeannette—he'd watch it again on TV, hoping to see his seven-year-old legs.

Jean Ehrenfried

"A few years ago, you and I, Ernest, you remember, before you sold Plou-Gouzan L'Ic, we went fishing. You'd bought some angling equipment you'd never used, and we set off to catch trout or carp or some other freshwater fish in a river near your house. As we walked along the path, we were absurdly happy. I'd never gone fishing and neither had you, unless you count foraging for crustaceans on the seashore. After half an hour, maybe less, you got a bite. You started hauling in your catch, wild with joy—I even think I helped you pull—and then a small, scared fish, wriggling at the end of the line, emerged into view. That fish scared us in turn. Ernest, you said to me, what should we do, what should we do? And I cried, let it go, let it go! You managed to free it from the hook and drop it back into the water. We packed up and left at once. On the way home, we were more or less stricken and didn't speak a word for a while. Then, all at once, you stopped and said: two titans."